Apparition
&
Late Fictions

Apparition
&
Late Fictions

A NOVELLA AND STORIES

Thomas Lynch

Jonathan Cape

London

Published by Jonathan Cape

2 4 6 8 10 9 7 5 3 1

First published in Great Britain in 2010 by
Jonathan Cape
Random House, 20 Vauxhall Bridge Road,
London SW1V 2SA

www.rbooks.co.uk

Addresses for companies within The Random House Group Limited can be found at:
www.randomhouse.co.uk/offices.htm

The Random House Group Limited Reg. No. 954009

A CIP catalogue record for this book
is available from the British Library

ISBN 9780224062190

Printed and bound in Great Britain by
CPI Mackays, Chatham, Kent ME5 8TD

This book is for
Mary Tata

Contents

Acknowledgments

THESE STORIES have been improved by the scrutiny of early readers including Mary Tata, George Martin, Tommy Lynch, Heather Grace Lynch, Nick Delbanco, Bret Lott, A. L. Kennedy, Keith Taylor, Richard McDonough, Sejal Sutaria, Pat Lynch, Dan Lynch, Michael Heffernan, George Bornstein, and Margaret Lazarus Dean, and by the guidance and good counsel of my editors, Jill Bialosky and Robin Robertson. For these, and for the assistance of Mike Lynch, Ken Kutzli and Sean Lynch, I am permanently grateful, as I am to the editors of the following journals where these stories first appeared, sometimes in different versions:

'Catch and Release' and 'Bloodsport' first appeared in *Witness*.

'Bloodsport' also appeared in *The Best American Mystery Stories 2001*, edited by Lawrence Block (Houghton Mifflin, 2001).

'Hunter's Moon' first appeared in *Granta*.

Acknowledgments

'Apparition' first appeared in a shorter version as 'Block Island' in *The Southern Review* and in the anthology *Not Safe, but Good: Stories Sharpened by Faith*, vol. 1, edited by Bret Lott (Thomas Nelson Books, 2007).

Apparition
&
Late Fictions

Catch and Release

THE THERMOS BOTTLE with his father's ashes in it rested on the front seat of the drift boat. He was glad to have the morning's busywork behind him and to be in the river. The green thermos with the silver cap looked inconspicuous enough.

Neither the waitress at the All Seasons Diner nor the other guides meeting their clients over biscuits and sausage gravy had noticed it. Nor had the woman from the tackle shop with whom he had arranged a car spot for his truck and trailer. He told her he'd be floating Walhalla to Custer and left her a set of keys. He took some twenty-pound shooting line, some ten-pound leader and eight-pound tippet, some split shot and a Snickers bar, some feathers and yarn. He'd been tying his own flies for years. 'On account', he told her, putting the gear on the counter.

'You'll be a long way downstream from the other guides,

Danny', she told him. 'Most of 'em are doing Green Cottage to Gleason's Landing. Salmon all over the gravel, they say. Or Gleason's to Bowman's or Rainbow to Sulac. No one's below Upper Branch but you.'

'That rain'll push some fresh one's in', he said. 'Some steelhead and lakeruns, maybe. First of October. It's time.'

'Well, you'll have some peace and quiet at least. It's a zoo up here with guides and canoes and walk-ins. Mind the bow hunters. Season opens today.'

'Peace and quiet, yes.'

He gathered his supplies and left.

Only Enid, the woman with whom he slept some nights, who managed his website and kept track of his bookings and packed his shore lunches, had been curious.

'What's with the thermos?' she'd asked when he stood in the door in the dark with his waders and vest. She knew he only drank Mountain Dew.

'A client's', he'd said, and bent to kiss her.

'Good luck', she whispered, and rolled over and returned to sleep. He pulled the quilt up over her bare shoulder. For a moment he wondered if he should stay.

AND PUSHING off from the Walhalla landing, in the first light of the first morning of the first October since his father died, with his lame dog Chinook curled in the boat's bow, his father's ashes in a thermos on the front seat, himself easing the oars into the downstream current – the three of them adrift in the Pere Marquette, the forest on either side of which was ablaze with the changes of Michigan's autumn – he thought it was nearly like taking his father fishing again and that the thermos bottle was a perfect camouflage and that he didn't know if such things ought to feel like weeping or like laughter. He loved the damp rotting smell of autumn, the breeze that bore it through the tunnel of the river, the pockets of fog, the marsh and mudbanks, the litter of fallen and falling trees, the unseen traffic in the woods, the distance his drift put between himself and all the other details and duties of ordinary time. He loved the snug hold of the river on his boat, the determination of its current, the certain direction, the quiet.

And though this time of year he could put sixty days of guiding together – from late August to late October – and though his arms and shoulders would burn from the rowing and his hands blister from the oars and ache from the tying of knots and his fingers would sting with line cuts and fish bites and embedded hooks, it never really seemed like work. But it was his work. Three hundred dollars a day, less 5 per cent for the lodge that booked the trip, less the cost of lunches and tackle and car spots, gas and gear, plus tips – these were the heydays of the year when yuppies from the suburbs all over the Midwest would drive their SUVs to Baldwin to dress up in their designer fly-fisherman costumes and catch the biggest fish of their lives on the lightest tackle. Danny took their pictures, took their money, filled them full of lore and stories, and sent them back to what he imagined were their trophy wives and dreary day jobs, glad that he had passed on all of that to become a trout bum and live the life he figured God intended him to live. This time of year, the only days of rest came from cancellations. The sales rep from Akron, booked for today, had called to say he couldn't get away.

◆   ◆   ◆

THE THERMOS had been his stepmother's idea. Though his father had been a minister all his life, and had officiated at hundreds of funerals, he had steadfastly refused to tell them what he wanted for his own arrangements. 'You'll know what to do', is all he'd ever say when questioned on the matter. 'Bury me or burn me or blow me out of a cannon – I don't care. I'll have my heaven. It's yours to do. That's one funeral I won't have to preach.'

So when it happened, it was Margaret, Danny's stepmother, who had decided that, after the wake and funeral, the body would be cremated. When his sister and brothers had questioned her, suggesting that he'd rather be buried at the family lot next to their mother, Margaret said it would make their father portable and divisible and, after all, he loved to travel and never got to do enough of it, and he always had tried to be fair with them all.

Thus, to his youngest son, the artist, she gave a portion of the ashes, which he mixed with acrylics and oils and began a series of portraits of his father. To his middle son, who was the associate pastor at the Presbyterian church, she gave a portion to be buried in a bronze urn under a tastefully diminutive stone in the local cemetery with his name and dates on it, next to his first wife. The graveside service, like the wake and funeral, was widely attended by fellow clergy, local Presbyterians, and townspeople. To his daughter she gave a portion sealed in a golden locket with an emerald on it which could be worn as a pendant or ankle bracelet in Ann Arbor where she practiced law. And to Danny she'd given the thermos – an old green Stanley one that looked like something carried by construction workers – and said, 'Why don't you take your father fishing?'

❖   ❖   ❖

DANNY REMEMBERED his father taking him fishing, that first time in the river, when he was a boy, how the water tightened around his body, the thick rubber of the Red Ball waders constricting in the current. It was late March. It was cold and clear and he wondered how his father ever found this place, hours from home, driving in the dark to get to the river at first light. How they stood overlooking the river from the top of the hill, its multiple interwoven channels his father called 'the Braids' because it was here the river split and turned and coiled around itself before returning to its orderly flow between two banks below Indian Bridge. He remembered his father saying they were going to a secret spot, back in the swamp, called Gus's Hole, named for the man who had discovered it and told someone who told someone who told Danny's father. Then hiking down the oak ridge with their rods and net and gear. His father held his hand as they stepped into the river and he could feel, for the first time, the weight of the water moving, something urgent and alive; and how his father held his hand high in the air, like dancers doing twirls through the deeper water, the boy he was then bobbing in the water, his father holding him aloft to keep the river from rushing over the top of his waders.

They fished hardware then – Little Cleos and Wobblers and other spoons that looked like wounded baitfish. Or clattering plugs that nose-dived in the current and jiggled just above the bottom. Later they would graduate to long poles and lighter tackle and various spinners. His father always swore by Mepps #4s with little egg-colored beads and copper blades. For steelhead they'd roll spawn bags through holes behind logjams and fallen trees and finally they gave up their spinning gear for fly rods and reels and the slow perfections of their own patterns – caddis and stoneflies and hex nymph variations – of preparation, presentation, catch and release.

But that first time Danny remembered nothing so much as the slow tug of the lure in the current, the fresh sensation of the river's bottom and the current's ways as he worked it through snags, over gravel, around stumps, and into the dark pools where his father told him fish were waiting. And he remembered the first fierce hit of the brown trout, how it rose in a fury and leapt and ran upstream, then downstream, taking line from the reel, and his father's calm counsel behind him, 'That's it, Danny, that's it', and the beauty of it in the net and the mystery of it and the sense that he had of having been chosen by the fish because he had made the long trip in the dark, endured the cold, and the long walk through the swamp to stand in the right spot and cast to the right place, and listened to his father's instructions and let the lure sink and work its way until it brought the eight-pound fish and the eight-year-old boy together.

Every winter, spring, and fall since then he'd fished the Pere Marquette – from mid-August to mid-October for the salmon's spawning run, until late December for the steelhead that would follow them to feast upon the eggs, then March and April for the spawning brown trout and steelhead. And long before Danny knew that the river had been named for a dead Jesuit missionary who'd died a couple of centuries before where the river emptied into Lake Michigan, long before he'd learned the names of birds and trees, waterfowl and wildflowers, he'd learned the habits of the river, its eddies and sluices, backwaters and rapids, its clay banks and sand and gravel bottoms, and the habits of the fish who spawned and lived and died in it. He knew the names of every hole and pocket and pool and gravel that was known for fish, from the Birch Hole to the Trestle Hole to Alligator Alley and the Aquarium, Hole 9, the Sand Hole, Wadels and the Highbanks, Beaver Den, the Improvements, the Maples, Stump's Lodge, and a hundred more, a fair few of which, unknown to anyone before himself, he had named. After a lackluster college career and half-hearted efforts working for General Motors as a driver at the Proving Grounds, he had taken his father's free advice to do something he was 'really truly passionate about.' He moved from the small house he shared with some high school friends to Baldwin, in western Michigan, near the river's headwaters, and resolved to be a trout bum. He guided in the fall and spring and went to Alaska or Montana in the summers and guided there. All winter he tied flies which he sold to the local outfitters and private buyers. He taught workshops for visiting executives, field-tested new gear for the manufacturers, worked his website and fished alone, studying the river, whenever he didn't have a client. It was enough to keep body and soul together. He was not yet thirty, never going to be rich, but was, nonetheless, among the most respected guides on the river, well known for what he knew that no one else knew better.

And though his father had given up winter fishing over the years, and would find excuses about the spring runs, they had shared the salmon and the autumn for twenty years. When his father loaned Danny the down payment on the cabin and ten acres of scrub pine west of town, he took in trade what he called a 'Life Lease' on the third week of September – the height of the season by his calculations.

This was the first year he never showed.

This was the September he had died instead. Something

'acute' and 'myocardial', the doctor had called it when Danny's father woke in the early morning, walked into the bathroom, and lay down on the green tile floor and died.

'He never said a word,' Danny's stepmother said, 'not a word. Never called out. Never made a sound.' Here she would pause and take a breath. 'It was as if he didn't want to disturb anyone, as if he knew it was his end.' She'd catch her breath again. 'A glass of water on the counter, a bottle of aspirin open, him on the floor, he never made a sound.'

THE DRIFT boat on the river never made a sound. Even the oars in the oarlocks were quiet. Danny could hear the fog lifting, the breeze and the leaf-fall, the wing flap of a heron lifting off. He could hear the water over the downed limbs of trees, under the riverbanks, the curl of a muskrat into the current. He could hear the winter oak and sumac and tag-elder and the air and his dog breathing and the perfect silence in the thermos. He wanted to scream.

He wanted to fill the elements with his heartache and anger – to shake a fist in the face of creation and ask God what exactly he had in mind that made his father die too soon. Why, when he was just at the point in his life when he could begin to enjoy it, after all the years of working for the church, out in the middle of the night when someone died, up in the morning to visit the sick or counsel the heartsore or balance the books, evenings with the deacons and the session, all those Saturday nights huddled in the office over his homily, lunching with locals, glad-handing the politicos. Why, after all those years of mortgage and tuition and car payments, always behind the eight ball on a churchman's stipend, always worried about the salvation of souls, the bricks and mortar; why, when he could finally begin to relax a little? Why now, why his father, why, goddamn it. Why?

But Danny shouted nothing into the woods. He only pushed the oars and worked the water to the first bend in the river, where he eased to the south bank, dropped the anchor, and stepped out of the boat. Chinook jumped from the bow into the water, up to the bank, and disappeared into the woods. The badly twisted left leg – he'd been hit by a car as a puppy – never slowed him down anymore. He'd learned to run with it and run without it when he turned up deer bedded down in the forest and chased them through the woods or rooted for voles in the undergrowth.

Danny pulled out his father's rod case, assembled the ten-foot eight-weight rod, attached his father's ancient reel, ran the line through the guides, and began to tie his terminal tackle.

'Your father would want you to have it', was what his step-mother had said, taking Danny to the basement back at home where the gear was kept. 'And he'd want your son to have it, if you ever have one.'

Danny couldn't imagine being a father. But for the first time it occurred to him that if he ever became a father, his children would never know their grandfather. This seemed wrong.

Danny had known *his* father's father. And had loved and admired the man who occupied his youth like a force of nature. He wondered if getting to heaven meant you got to ask these reasonable questions. Why? How? When? Why not?

He opened his father's fly box.

He felt his face tighten around his eyes. He began to weep.

It was not the bone-wracking sob he'd been holding back for

months now, ever since the morning he'd gotten word. It was not the shoulder-shaking, wind-robbing breakdown with his name on it he knew he'd have to have eventually. It was only the catch in his breath and the tightening behind his eyes and the improbable twitching of his eyebrows at the sight of his father's little collection of caddis and stonefly patterns, some streamers, eggs in different colors. But it was not so much the flies as the knots, the bits of line like little hangman's knots in the eye of each hook where his father had bitten them off after they hadn't produced or after a day's fishing or after they'd produced enough. His father had never learned more than two knots. The nail knot for leader and tippet and the cinch knot for flies. Danny had brought home wonderful variants from the Katmai Lodge in Alaska where the salmon ran to fifty pounds and from the cutthroat waters in Colorado and Montana. But his father never wanted to learn them. He trusted his tying and never lost a fish, he was fond of affirming, on account of knots. His held, he'd insisted, however old-fangled.

Danny wiped his eyes, glad that he was fishing the low water, glad for the little release, glad for the feel of his father's knots as he bit one off a yellow egg and tied it freshly to his line.

The water had risen with last night's rain and darkened some and the sun was not yet high enough to see into the hole but he knew this bend by heart and reckoned the fish would be suspended in it and tied one split shot on and cast it back-hand slightly upstream toward the opposite bank. He could feel the split shot in the gravel at the top of the hole, and could feel it fall into the deeper run, and he watched the loop in his line straighten in the current and held the rod out in front of him as the line moved through the water. At the bottom of the run he began to strip back line and looped it out upstream again, the familiar balance between fisherman and rod tip and terminal tackle establishing a cadence to the casting, the fly's drift, and the retrieval so that he was covering the hole every thirty seconds. He avoided, in his cast, the bronze leaves of an overhanging oak tree, and in his drift, the submerged stump at the bottom of the run. He could hear Chinook deep in the forest rolling in something dead and rotting. Part wolf, part malamute, he could not help himself, Danny thought.

On his eighth or tenth cast, the fly stopped early in the run and Danny set the hook and a huge buck king salmon rose shaking its head to the surface. Yes! he could hear himself saying to himself as he felt the first surge of the fish against him. This was always new, always the first time, never routine, this wonder that two separate natures could intersect like this. The fish roiled on the surface, dove deep into the hole, and held there, the line pulsing, rod pulsing with the weight of it, then it ran upstream toward the logjam above the gravel, taking line off the reel as it worked its way. The look Danny got of it in the shallows made him guess, eighteen, twenty, maybe twenty-one pounds. And it was fresh – silver and blue – only out of the lake a couple of days, still weeks away from spawning and fatigue and death. Danny loved the ferocity of fish in the lower water. He could see the tiny egg in the bony upper jaw. Right in the snot-locker, he could hear himself saying, and turned to look, because he'd never in all these years gotten out of the habit of turning to look for his father's amazement and excitement and approval. But there was no one grabbing for the camera or the video cam or the net or anything. There was only the boat snug to the riverbank and the thermos bottle on the front seat and Danny, momentarily disconnected from the fish's struggle, failed to turn the fish back downstream, and in the lapse the salmon got under the logjam and, free of the reel's drag and the rod's wisdom, it snapped the eight-pound tippet easily. Danny felt the line go limp, he could see the fish jump behind the logjam, his father's egg pattern still in its jaw. He turned and looked back to the boat. There was nothing. He was alone. For the first time since his father's dying he felt his father's death, the dull, undeniable force of it, and it dropped him to his knees in the river, the water nearly running over the top of his chest waders, its cold embrace a kind of comfort as his body shook in spasms. He held his father's fishing rod aloft as the weight of the river beat against his chest. The fog was lifting now; the morning warming as the sun rose. He whistled for Chinook, stood, and walked back to the boat.

Standing beside the boat in the water, he reached for the thermos on the front seat, unscrewed the stainless steel top that served as a coffee cup, set it on the bow. Then he loosened the cap in the mouth of the thing and poured a handful of his father's ashes into his right hand. They were dull gray and sharp-edged and utterly dry. They had about them the feel of vermiculite or kitty litter or something freeze-dried that could, with the addition of water, be reconstituted. He grinned at the prospect that 'just adding water' might bring his father back. He let his hand drop into the river, where he opened his fist and released the ashes into the current. The little white puff, like a cloud of milt when the buck salmon spawn, disappeared downstream.

Danny waited for something like an overwhelming feeling, and when none was forthcoming, he recapped the thermos, climbed back in the boat, weighed his anchor, and eased into the downstream current. He found himself sighing, breathing deeply, grinning inexplicably.

Chinook kept up through the woods, chasing along the riverbank, sometimes leaping in the river to swim beside the boat or behind it or crossing in front of it like a furry dolphin. He'd climb the bank on the other side and rummage among the overgrowth for muskrat and squirrels and possum. Long ago he'd learned to run with the twisted left leg, and when he needed the most speed, when he'd kick deer out of their bedding, to simply tuck it up and run on three legs. Danny reckoned it never slowed him down but kept him from going too far astray. Never out of earshot, a whistle from Danny would bring the dog to the riverbank to check in; then he would disappear again into the deep green of the forest. The dog stayed tuned to the sound of the boat and to his master's noises. Danny was glad he hadn't killed the thing.

He'd only just gotten the dog a few years before. He'd chosen him from a litter in Alaska, his first season there, and brought him home with him to Michigan. Unaccustomed to traffic that would not stop, the dog had run into a street in Mount Pleasant, where Danny had been partying with old college friends, and was hit by a car taking an old couple to the casino. They felt horrible. They offered to pay for any treatment. Danny had taken the dog to the vet, who suggested the veterinary school at Michigan State University. The dog was sedated and Danny raced to East Lansing, where student vets set the leg, put it in a cast, and thanked Danny for his confidence in them. When the cast came off, Chinook's leg was badly twisted. Another vet suggested a surgeon in Chicago. Danny drove the dog there and the surgeon, taking a look at the damages, told Danny he'd really be better off putting the dog down. The leg, he said, would never be right. The older Chinook got the more it would be in the way. He could, of course, remove the leg and the dog might even get on without it. Other dogs did. But a three-legged dog? The surgeon said he could euthanize Chinook.

He'd called his father. His father said that he trusted Danny's instincts. He said he knew that Danny would know the right thing to do. He said he admired him for taking on the care of the dog and these difficult decisions. His father had told him to say his prayers, to listen to God, and the right thing would come to him, whatever it was. He told Danny to take a day or two to think it over. He told him he'd be willing to help, whatever the decision was.

Danny rowed past the first confluence. The sun was working up the sides of the trees. The day was going to be blue. He found himself talking to his father's ashes.

Let go, let God, he heard himself saying.

He was thinking of that first brown trout. He remembered wanting to take it home to show his mother. His father said they could either take it home and it would die and they would eat it or they could let it go. His father was working the lure out of its jaw. Danny was holding the handle of the net the fish was flopping in. He couldn't believe the options. Kill it, eat it, show his mother. Let it go. Never see it again. It was so beautiful. How could he let it go. How could he kill it. He remembered how it made him feel cold, for the first time, having to make such an awful choice.

At the second confluence, the river turned westward and the topography flattened and the current slowed into an area all of the guides called 'the Serengeti', because it was a large flat expanse of cat marsh a mile wide on either side of the main flow. Surrounded by a high ridge of ancient white pines, winter oaks and sugar maples, the area seemed like a huge bowl of natural wonders. Whenever his father fished this float with him, he'd always call it a National Geographic moment when they'd make their way into the Serengeti. Once they'd seen a pair of fully matured bald eagles and a young eagle with them in a tree. They'd seen osprey and owls and plenty of heron, and in one shallow backwater slough, outside the current, they'd seen salmon by the thousands milling about, as if resting from the furious pursuit of reproduction and mortality that had triggered their return to the river. The irony of this discovery was that these were literally fish in a barrel, but because there was no current, there was no way to present a fly to them in a way that would induce them to strike it. Danny and his father could only row in and out among the hordes of fish remarking on nature's strange abundance.

After the Serengeti the boat bearing Danny and his dog and his father's ashes drifted into the Braids. This was a maze of river and stream and rivulet that from overhead might look like a bunch of pretzels. It was rarely fished because guides could get lost in it, following the wrong shoot to its dead end, at which point the boat would have to be walked out against the current, or circling some loop outside of the mainstream. Local meat fishermen used to hike in with burlap bags and clear out a hole with weighted snagging hooks on thick line and stiff rods. But the DNR had impounded a pickup and a bunch of gear some years before, so even the snaggers left the swamp alone now. No fish was worth the loss of a truck.

Danny remembered, as a boy, fishing Gus's Hole with his father, when a pair of snaggers appeared in the hole just above the one he and his dad were fishing. He could hear the boozy laughter and the splash of the treble hook and the line ripping through the water as they yanked and yanked until the hook lodged in the belly or the side or the tail of a salmon. He could hear the leap and splash of the foul-hooked fish and the shouting of the snaggers, how they'd hoot and howl and they'd crank the huge reels and how the short stiff rods seemed like baseball bats and how they'd take ten fish out of a hole, then move on through the swamp.

At the Sand Hole, a twenty-yard expanse between fallen cedars, Danny tied a single egg on. He stood above the hole, cast quarter down, sweeping the red, above the hen salmon he could see fanning the gravels with her tail, the males lined up like a squadron behind her. A pocket of dark water the width of a dining-room table seemed to suck the egg into its deeper habitats. As the egg worked its way into the sweet spot where the current and seam and the foam line converged, he let out line so the fly would sink. Here was where he figured the steelhead held – where the O_2 was highest, the food flow was fastest, and the deeper water gave them cover, downstream from the spawning salmon and browns. All the fanning of the gravel would send a constant buffet of hex nymph and stoneflies and caddis along with fresh spawn from the maturing salmon. He imagined the steelhead, mouth agape, holding in the current, gulping anything that looked like protein floating by. On his second cast, the fish slammed the egg with such ferocity Danny lurched forward, set his foot, then set the hook. The water broiled and he could see the pale white mouth of the huge rainbow which dove deep, then rocketed out of the water, then dove and ran downstream, jumping twice, then turning back so fast the line slackened and Danny reeled as fast as he could. From wherever he was in the woods, Chinook could hear the line peeling against the drag, the fat smacking of the fish on the water, Danny shouting 'Yes! Yes!' and ran to witness the commotion. It was fifteen minutes before the huge silver fish, fifteen pounds of hunger and outrage, was backed into the shallows where Danny held his line tight, the rod aloft, and, genuflecting, grabbed the steelhead by its tail. The tiny hook was deeply embedded in its jaw and with a pair of forceps Danny worked the hook free, held the gasping, wriggling fish to his face, admiring its teeth, its steely eyes, then knelt in the water and worked it back and forth in the current, letting the water wash through its gills, restoring the spent thing's equilibrium. After thirty or forty seconds of this, he could feel the fish's muscles flexing, Danny loosened his hold of the huge tail just enough for the fish to sense freedom. In a flash it was gone.

It was his favorite thing – to hunt the stealthy, transparent, invisible fish, to know enough about its habits to isolate it in all that dark water, to present a fly or an egg of his own making, the right size and color, at the right angle at the right depth at the right speed to trigger the thing to animal desire, then to fight the thing in its own environs, counting on his knots, his timing, and the proper setting of his drag, then to catch the thing, to hold it, and then to let it go.

'Love 'em and leave 'em', is what his father used to say, and it was true. No dinner of salmon or steelhead, and they'd had plenty, ever made him feel as full as the utter mastery involved with returning the captive to its freedom, the genuine pleasure of letting it go.

Among his clients it was well known now that Danny would put you on fish, teach you to catch fish, work hard to net them, and take your picture with them. And you could keep one male chinook or coho to take home to barbecue for the neighbors, with too much beer and blathermentia, but whatever plenty the season provided, whatever the limit the State of Michigan allowed, one salmon was the limit on Danny's boat and none was better and no browns or steelhead were ever kept.

'But they're all just going to die', one of his clients once protested when Danny released a thirty-pound hen.

'We're all just going to die', Danny told him, 'sooner or later, a hundred per cent.'

Danny washed the fish slime off his hands, poured another handful of his father's ashes out, kissed the fist he held them in, and let them go into the dark water.

He sat with his dog on the bank for a few minutes, waiting for no particular reason, watching the salmon working the reds. Everything around him seemed a metaphor for his father – the leaf-fall, the clear water, the fish in their futile quest. He tried to remember when he first became aware that his father approved of him, his life, and whether it was a gift outright or whether he had earned it.

Early on they'd argued over church and Sundays. He'd quit after his mother died. He was ten when she had died of 'complications' involving 'medications' and 'depression'. And though he would stand in the first pew on the left side of the church with his stepmother and siblings – for his father had married Margaret within the year – with a hymnal in his hand for a few years after that, he was never really 'there' and didn't really sing the songs or believe or understand the light that came through stained glass or how it had happened – how or why his mother had been removed from their lives. At thirteen he simply refused to go and gave his father and Margaret to believe that if forced he'd make a scene that would embarrass them more than his absence. He took to fishing Sundays at the dam below the park in town for bluegill and crappie and sucker and carp. He'd learned to like the quiet and the privacy and the feel of fish on the other end of his line. And when he told his father years later that the river, the Pere Marquette, was his church and chapel and Bible and choir, that he felt closer to God there and closer to himself there and closer to his mother there and closer to life, his father had nodded, if not approval, then at least acceptance. 'The Lord', the churchman told his son, 'has a fondness for fishermen.' This was near enough to forgiveness.

And there'd been issues over education. Danny had been a lackluster student. After high school he'd managed to get accepted to Central Michigan University. It was the nearest school to Baldwin and the Pere Marquette. He enrolled in a course of General Studies, but between the draw of the Indian casino on the edge of town and the Pere Marquette less than two hours away, nothing in the curriculum could keep his interest for long. Whenever he could he'd drive to the river and float a stretch, researching the pocket water, the structure and the habits of resident and migrant fish. Home for Easter that first year, Danny's father told him he could not succeed by doing things halfway.

'Do something you're really passionate about. What's the worst that can happen? You're young. You can afford to fail but you can't afford not to *try*.'

This was permission enough for Danny. He quit school. Worked on a landscape crew for three months, and with the cash bought a tent, three new Orvis rods and Billy Pate reels, and moved to Baldwin in early August, with his drift boat outfitted, pitching his tent on the river, where he slept and tied flies when he wasn't fishing. He'd begun hanging out at the PM Lodge and the local bars and tackle shops, picking up guide trips where he could. It wasn't long before word got around about his talents for putting clients on fish, for finding the right drift through difficult holes, for working the river in difficult conditions. Some fishing guides were taxi drivers. Rowing to some famous meat hole and sitting tight all day, then rowing out. Danny fished the slots and shoeboxes, the lesser-known pools where fish held on deep gravel or between difficult snags and stumps. He'd taught himself what shade did and rain did and the moon did to the habits of fish and the conduct of water.

When he climbed back in the boat, Chinook bolted downstream, then into the forest. Danny pulled the anchor up and felt the current's slow embrace circle the boat and take it in. He dipped his oars. The thermos, now nearly empty, rolled slightly on the front seat.

As he approached Gus's Hole Danny whistled for his dog. He anchored in the current and listened close. Sometimes his heart filled with the beauty and the silence of the place. Deep in the swamp, beyond the energies of other guides and walk-ins, the sense of isolation and privacy was comforting. And Gus's Hole itself held few fish anymore. The current had changed enough over the years to widen and flatten out the confluence of water. Still the area was fishy and the air was full of the smell of rotting salmon and the sickly-sweet smell of some larger putrefaction in the woods. Danny reckoned it was a deer shot out of season by a bow hunter who couldn't trail it through the swamp. In the distance he could hear Chinook howling. He whistled again and waited. After five minutes he could hear the dog approaching.

Danny wondered if the dog knew how close it had come to being killed in this place. It was to Gus's Hole Danny had brought the dog two years before, after all the experts had weighed in with their advice. They'd fished all day and Danny climbed the high banks to the oak ridge from which he and his father had first looked down on the curling braids of river that formed the swamp that winter years ago when he was eight. He had a field shovel and a pistol he had borrowed from a fellow guide. At the top, he began digging the dog's grave, the work quickening with anger and slowing with sadness, the variable speeds of the labor like the division of his heart. He had the grave dug, the pistol loaded, the blanket he intended to wrap the corpse in ready. He whistled for the dog and called 'Chinook!' He heard the dog bark and saw, from the high ridge, the dog emerge from a marshy island a quarter of a mile downstream. 'C'mon, Chinook', Danny called, and the dog ran the bank upstream fifty yards, then dove into the current, crossing to a sandbar in the middle, shook himself dry, then dove again, swimming upstream fifty more yards before coming to the base of the high banks. He shook himself dry again and bounded up the steep hill without slowing. At the top of the high banks he leapt into Danny's embrace. This prodigious bit of cross-country swimming and sprinting and climbing, regardless of the crookedness of his leg, proved the dog well able for his habitat. It convinced Danny that he should not kill him, not now, not ever, unless he was truly pained or endangered by his handicap.

And when his father heard, he had approved. 'Surely', he had said, 'we must tolerate some imperfections in the ones we love.'

Two years later the dog's 'imperfection' hadn't held him back a bit.

Danny sat on the bank and shook the thermos. There was maybe a cup of his father's ashes left in it. He wondered what to do. The river had its share of him, working its way now, Danny reckoned, downstream to Scottville and Ludington and out into the big lake and maybe to the mouth of the Chicago River and into the Mississippi and through the middle ground of America into the Gulf of Mexico, to the larger amalgam of oceans that held the continents afloat on the globe.

He poured the remnant into the silver cap of the thermos. He dipped the thermos into the current and poured the cold water into the capful of ashes. With his knife he mixed the water and the ashes into a kind of gray paste, like thick oatmeal, and then he ate it with a spoon.

Bloodsport

M OST TIMES the remembrance was triggered by color – that primary red of valentines or Coca-Cola ads – the color of her toenails, girlish and perfectly polished. He remembered her body, tiny and lifeless and sickeningly still as she lay opened and autopsied on the prep-room table. He could still bring to mind, these many years since, the curl of the knot in the viscera bag the pathologist had tied, with all of her examined organs inside, and the raw edge of the exit wound in her right leg and the horrible precision of the hole in her breast where the man who murdered her put the muzzle of the gun.

And he remembered the dull inventory of detail, the hollow in her mother's voice the morning she called him at the funeral home.

'Elena's been shot, Martin. Up in Baldwin. She's at the Lake County Morgue. Go and get her, Martin. Bring her home.'

✦　　✦　　✦

ELENA HAD been only fifteen when her father died – the darkly beautiful daughter of a darkly beautiful mother and a man who'd had cancer. He was laid out in an 18-gauge metal casket. The funeral was huge. Martin could remember standing between them, Elena and her widowed mother, when they'd come to see the dead man's body. He figured he was ten years older than the daughter, ten years younger than the mother. He had asked, as he'd been trained to ask, if everything was 'satisfactory.' It was the failure of words that always amazed him.

'He got so thin.'
'Yes.'
'At least he's not suffering anymore.'
'No.'

'Thank you, Martin.'
'Yes.'

And he remembered how Elena, after trying to be brave for her mother, after standing and staring at the lid of the casket as if she could tough it out, as if she could look but not see, had let her gaze fall on the face of her dead father and cried, in one great expiration of pain, 'Oh Daddy! Please, no', and nearly doubled over at the middle, holding her tummy, and how her knees buckled and how he grabbed her before she fell to the floor. And how she had pressed her sobs into his shirt and how he'd hugged her close and felt her holding on and could smell her hair and feel the form and perfect sadness in her shaking body and how he'd said that everything would be all right because he really didn't know what to say. It made him feel necessary and needed and he wanted to hold her and protect her and make everything better, because she was beautiful and sad and though he could not fix it he would not let her go until she could stand on her own two feet again. And he thought that being the only embalmer in town was no bad thing when you stood among the widowed and orphaned and they would thank you for the unhappy work you'd done on their people.

FIVE YEARS after that and it was Elena, killed by her husband with a gun.

Martin could not get his mind off how mannish the violence was, how hunter-gatherly, how very do-it-yourself, for the son-of-a-bitch, according to the coroner, to stand on the front deck of their double-wide out in the woods while she loaded the last of her belongings in the car – her boom box and a last armful of hanging things – how he must have carefully leveled the rifle, his eyes narrowing to sight her in. He put the first bullet through her thigh. An easy shot from fifteen yards.

He must have wanted to keep her from running.

'The way you would with any wild thing', the fat pathologist, smelling of stale beer, had told Martin in the morgue, taking the cigar out of his mouth to hold forth like an expert. 'You hobble it first, then you don't have to chase a blood trail through the woods all night.' He warmed to his subject. 'Bow hunters go for the heart or lungs most times. They don't mind chasing through swamps and marshes after a wounded buck. It's part of the sport to them. But shooters go for the head or the legs.'

And as she lay in the thick leaf-fall beside the car, bleeding from the severed femoral artery, he'd walked over, put the barrel to her left breast, and squeezed off another round.

'She'd have bled to death either way', the pathologist said. The sight of that fat hand with the cigar touching the spot on Elena's thigh where the bullet tore its exit out sickened Martin. And when the same hand pulled the sheet back to show the terrible carnage to her torso – the postmortem incisions very loosely stitched up and the black and blue and red little wound where her killer must have reckoned her heart would be, Martin quickly moved his stretcher beside the morgue tray, covered her body, and took charge before the pathologist carried his feckless lecture any further. He signed the logbook beside Elena's name and case number, got the death certificate marked *Gunshot wounds to leg and chest* in the section that asked for the cause of death and *Homicide* where it asked for manner and had her name and date of death, all of it scrawled in the sloppy hand of the pathologist, and got her out of there.

All the way home he tried to imagine how it must have happened – if anyone could have heard it, the small-caliber outrage of it, as if she'd been a doe feeding among the acorns or come to the salt lick, her large brown eyes full of panic and stillness. He wondered if she knew he was dangerous. He wondered if she realized, after the first shot, that he was going to kill her. He wondered if she died with fear or resolve. He wondered if, bleeding from the first wound, she might have passed out, and never saw the face of her killer or the barrel or the gun or felt it on her body or saw his eyes as he pulled the trigger.

Taken as a thing itself, considered within the broad range of human conduct, undistracted by his professional duties, Martin regarded the aberration of the dead girl's body riding behind him as utterly incomprehensible. How could someone kill someone so coldly, someone with whom you had made plans, had sex, watched television, promised love? It left him with a functional ambiguity. Martin tried to assemble a reasonable sentence in which the last phrase went like *and then he shot her, twice, because* . . . but he was always unsuccessful.

He looked in the rearview mirror at the length of the stretcher in the back of the hearse with its tidy blue cover under which Elena's body was buckled in, her head on the pillow, a small bag with her bloodied clothes, her jewelry and personal effects beside her. He tried to connect this horror with his remembrance of a sad, beautiful girl sobbing at the graveside of her dead father a few years before, waiting for the priest to finish with his prayers. The morning was blue and sunlit, the buds of maples just busting loose, the men who'd been pallbearers lined up on one side of the grave, Elena and her mother and grandmother on the other. And all around, a couple hundred people who'd come to pay their respects – women who worked with Elena's mother at the real estate office, men who worked with her father at the shop, parishioners from Our Lady of Mercy and kids from the freshman class of the high school. And after the priest had finished, Martin had nodded to the pallbearers to remove their gloves and solemnly place them on the casket – a little gesture of letting go. And then, from the pile of dirt next to the grave, under the green grass matting, he'd given a small handful of dirt, first to the dead man's mother, then to the dead man's wife, and then to Elena; and at his direction, each stepped up to the casket and traced a cross on the top with the dirt that Martin had given them. He put a hand on their elbows as they stepped on the boards in a gesture of readiness and ever-vigilant assistance. And after that, Martin made the announcement he had practiced saying out loud the night before.

'This concludes the services for Mr. Delano.'

He reminded himself to speak slowly, to enunciate, to articulate, to project.

'The family wishes to thank each of you for your many kindnesses – for the floral tributes and Mass cards and most especially for your presence with them this morning.'

He took a breath, tried to remember what part came next.

'You are all invited to return now to Our Lady of Mercy Parish Hall where a luncheon has been prepared in Mr. Delano's memory. You may step now directly to your cars.'

At this direction, people began to move away, relieved at the end of the solemnities, talking freely, trading news and sympathies. Martin had been pleased with the performance. Everything had gone off just as he'd planned – a fitting tribute, a good funeral. The pallbearers walked away as a group, looking official. Someone assisted the grandmother from the grave. Elena's mother, her eyes tired and red, took Martin's arm as they walked to the limousine, holding the rose Martin had given her, the crowd of people parting as they made their way. And Martin was thinking this is no bad thing for people to see what a dependable man their new funeral director was – a reliably upright, lean-on-me kind of man – less than a year out of mortuary school, mortgaged to the eyes for the business he'd bought from the widow of the man who'd been here before, but clearly a responsible, dependable citizen, someone to be called on, night or day, if there was trouble.

At the door to the car Mrs. Delano stopped, turned toward Martin with a brave smile, tilted her head slightly, opened her arms, and Martin, sensing that she wanted him to, without hesitation bent to embrace her. She was saying 'Thank you, Martin' and 'I could never have made it through this without you' loud enough for bystanders to hear and he was patting her back professionally, all caring and kindness as you would with any hurt or wounded fellow human, saying to her, 'You did good, he'd be proud of you', and she was patting his shoulders, and then, once the hug was over, holding the hankie to her eyes, she quickly disappeared into the backseat of the car in a rush of grief and relief and gratitude, and Martin straightened up and held the door.

Elena, who'd been following Martin and her mother to the limousine, holding two roses she'd picked from her father's casket spray, paused at the car door and, perhaps because she was following her mother's lead, perhaps thinking it was the proper thing to do, looked Martin in the eyes and said, 'Thank you, thank you for everything', and reached up to lock her hands around Martin's neck, and just as Martin was starting to say, in a voice all caring and kindness, 'You're very welcome, Elena', she rose on her tiptoes, pressed her body firmly against his, and kissed him squarely on the mouth. Martin could feel her chest on his chest, her small hands holding the sides of his face, and her soft mouth opening slightly and the wetness of it on his lips. He let go of the door handle and held her at the waist, first pulling her toward him, then, opening his eyes, gently pushing her away, and when she stopped kissing him, he could feel his face reddening and he was wondering if the priest and the pallbearers and the townspeople could see his blush and the flash of desire he could feel in himself and the wish beginning to form in his mind that everyone would disappear so that he could hold her and touch her and comfort her and have her and then, but before he could pat her on the back professionally, before he could say, 'There, there, everything is going to be all right', before he had a chance to restore the air of solemnity and order, Elena proffered, with a brave smile, one of the roses she was holding. He took it from her and, as her mother had, Elena disappeared headfirst into the back of the long black Cadillac.

For weeks afterwards Martin had tried to figure that kiss, its meaning. Surely she could not have known how much he might have imagined, after holding her at her father's casket, her sweetness and innocence and beauty and vulnerability and how much a man like Martin felt like protecting and consoling and holding and touching her. Surely he'd been discreet, during the long hours of visitation at the funeral home, standing at the back of the chapel watching Elena and her mother greeting the neighbors and family and friends who came. She could hardly have any idea of her own beauty, the perfect form, her small arms, her lithe body, her dark eyes, her breasts, the softness of her walking. Martin had been determined to look professional, caring, concerned. He had made an effort not to stare. Surely it was only that she was overwhelmed with the graveside duties, the deep emotions, or having seen her mother embrace Martin, and awkward about the currencies of thanks and the conventions of familiarity, she had overstated her gratitude, overpaid her sense of indebtedness. Or maybe in some way that Martin could not sort out entirely, the attachment to her father, torn apart by his untimely dying, was looking for another 'male' attachment? Martin remembered a movie he'd seen in which a young widow whose husband gets killed in World War II takes a teenage boy into her bed, in her grief. Yes, love and grief, maybe something complex like that.

◆   ◆   ◆

THERE WAS a safety in dealing with only the parts – the arteries and chemistries, the closure of eyes and lip lines, the refitting of cranium and sternum, the treatment of cavities and viscera, the placement of hands, the suturing of wounds and incisions, the rouge and lipstick and nail polish, the dressing and hairdo and casketing. Duty had a way of separating Martin from what it was he was doing. Stuffing the opened cranium with cotton, fitting the skullcap back in place and easing the scalp back over the skull, thereby restoring the facial contours, and minding the tiny stitches from behind one ear to behind another was only part of the process of embalming; and embalming was only part of the process of laying out the dead, which was only part of the process of the funeral, and the funeral was only a part of the larger concept of a death in the family, and a death in the family was a more manageable prospect, more generic, somehow, than the horror – round and witless and recognizable and well beyond his professional abilities – of a lovely girl, grown lovelier as a woman, who leaned on him and counted on him and had kissed him once as if she meant it and who moved away and then got shot like an animal in the woods by a man about whom Martin knew next to nothing.

FOR MONTHS after her father's funeral, Martin kept an eye out for Elena. Her mother came to pay the bill, and pick up more holy cards and thank-you notes. And then she came to order a stone. *Beloved Husband and Father*, is what it said. Martin had advised her against a double marker. She was young and would surely remarry, he thought.

And Martin would always ask, 'How is Elena doing?' in his most professional, caring voice.

'She's having some trouble with her schoolwork. She doesn't sleep well. I'm a little worried.'

Martin gave Elena's mother a list of grief support groups, run by the local hospice and area churches. He reminded her that there used to be 'a year of mourning' and said that Elena's feelings were probably 'very normal' and that 'time heals all wounds'.

'Yes', said Elena's mother. 'It's just so hard.'

She thanked Martin again for everything and said she hoped he'd understand if she said she hoped she wouldn't be seeing him again.

Martin smiled and nodded and said he understood completely.

THE NEXT June, Martin read in the local paper how Elena had been captain of the debate team that went to the regional finals in Ann Arbor, and the year after that she had gone to Italy on a Rotary Exchange Scholarship, and in her senior year she was pictured on the front page smiling in her prom dress beside the son of the man who owned the Lincoln Mercury dealership in town, over a caption that read *A Night to Remember*, and Martin remembered how very happy she looked, how very sweet. After that he pretty much lost track of her.

'AFTER HER father died', Elena's mother told Martin when she came in to pick out a casket and arrange the funeral, 'she seemed a little lost.'

Martin listened and nodded as Elena's mother, looking so much older now, outlined the details of her dead daughter's life. She'd finished school, applied to college, spent the summer after graduation waitressing in a bar-restaurant in western Michigan, to get out on her own and earn a little money.

'She met him there. At the Northwoods Inn.'

He worked for the county road commission and came in week nights after work and weekends after fishing or hunting. He was handsome and chatty. He had a trailer in the woods. He gave her compliments and brought her flowers and bought her beer and cheeseburgers. And when it came time to go to university, to get the education her father had saved for, she called her mother and told her that she was moving in with this man.

'I didn't approve, but what could I do, Martin? Her father would never have allowed it. But what could I do?'

Martin shook his head and nodded.

'I told her she was throwing her life away on a summer fling, but she said she loved him. She loved him and he killed her, shot her like a damn dog, Martin.'

Elena's mother's sobs grew heavy. Martin poured her a glass of water, moved the box of Kleenex nearer to her.

'Thank you, Martin', she said. 'I'm sorry.'

'Not at all', he said. 'It's okay.'

'In no time she was pregnant and he said he wanted to "do right" by her. I told her he would always feel trapped, or always feel like he had done her a big favor, always feel like he was such a big man and she was just nothing without him, but she said she loved him and maybe it was all meant to happen like this and what could I do, Martin? What could I do? Her father would have gone up there and brought her home, but I had no one, no one.'

They were married in the county offices in a civil ceremony,

Elena wearing her prom dress and her new husband wearing a cowboy hat and a blue jean jacket and a string tie.

Elena's mother took the wedding snapshot out of her purse and told Martin to 'cut him off of there and use that picture for the paper and the holy cards. She was so happy then.'

Elena miscarried in her third month and took a job working dispatch for the Sheriff's Office.

By the following midsummer things were getting bad. Her husband's appetite for Budweiser and bloodsport hadn't abated.

'She'd call home crying, Martin. He still went to the bar week nights. He'd come home boozy and, well, unpredictable. And he spent the weekends tramping through the woods shooting small game, which he'd bring home for her to clean and cook.'

He'd go out at night and snag spawning salmon and bring them back to freeze and smoke and put up in jars.

'Her letters home got so sad, Martin – "He doesn't bathe enough", she wrote me once, "he seems so angry"'.

She had taken from her purse a packet of pink envelopes and was holding them and rocking a little in the chair across the desk from Martin.

'She had such beautiful handwriting.'

Martin nodded, smiled, understood.

'She called me crying horribly once and I asked her if he'd hit her but she said no, no. He had killed a fawn, right outside their trailer. It had come with its mother to feed at the pile of carrots he baited them with. They were in bed. Sunday morning. He sat up, walked to the window, went to the door where he kept his rifle. It was months before the legal season. He shot it right from the door. The fawn, Martin. The little fawn.'

She was shaking now again, sobbing and rocking in the chair.

'Do you know what he told her, when she yelled at him for shooting the fawn?'

Martin shook his head.

'He told her it couldn't live without its mother anyway.'

Now she was sobbing and shaking fitfully and Martin reached across the desk to take hold of her hands, in which she held the packet of her daughter's letters.

'We don't have to do this now', Martin told her.

But she wanted to go on, to get it out, to get this part behind her.

AFTER HE killed the baby deer, Elena applied to the state university in Mount Pleasant using the return address at the Sheriff's Office. When the letter came from the admissions department, beginning *Dear Ms. Delano: Congratulations!* she made a copy and mailed it home with a note asking her mother if there was still money left for her education.

'"Of course", is what I told her', Elena's mother told Martin. 'I wanted her to get her education before she settled down. After she lost the baby, she had no reason to stay with him. And he was drinking and depressed. He worked and drank and grew more distant. She could see she had made a big mistake. I could tell she wasn't happy.'

Elena told her mother how she gave her husband back his leather coat and the tiny diamond ring and said she would always care about him but that she had been too young and she felt she owed it to her father to return to school and get her life on track and she would always treasure their time together but she really had to go. She thought it would be the best thing for them both. She was sure he wasn't happy either.

The night before she had planned to leave, she did her hair and polished her nails and cooked him pheasant and they ate by candlelight – 'for old times' sake', she had told her mother when she called to say she'd be home tomorrow. She really wanted no hard feelings. It had been her mistake and she was sorry to have involved him in it. Surely they would always be friends.

'He's okay with it. He doesn't like it but he's okay with it', is what she told her mother when her mother asked her how he was taking it.

And, near as the coroner and the sheriff could piece it together, it was after everything she owned had been loaded in the car, the trunk full of books and photo albums, the backseat packed with her stereo and a rack of hanging clothes and the front passenger seat with the one suitcase full of toiletries and socks and underwear; maybe she was turning to wave goodbye before going, or maybe he'd been drinking Budweiser all night, or maybe he'd helped her and then went berserk, but whatever happened, whether it was passion or calculation, before she sat into the driver's seat, he got the rifle from wherever he kept it, and near as they could figure by the angle of the wound, he stood on the front porch, aimed, and fired, then walked over to where she lay in the leaf-fall beside the car and shot her again, in the breast.

This was the part that Martin could never imagine – the calculation of shooting her in the leg, then slowly, deliberately walking over and pressing the barrel against her left breast and pulling the trigger. Wouldn't such madness in a man give signs before? Wouldn't the first gunshot wake him from the dream?

Elena's mother was rocking in the chair across from Martin, sobbing quietly, clutching the letters, staring at the snapshot of her daughter on the desk standing next to the man who had just killed her.

'You pick out the casket, Martin. I can't do it. Something like her father's. Please, Martin. You do it.'

He used the cherry casket with the moss pink velvet interior, and though it was considerably more costly than what Elena's father was buried in, he charged the same and thought it was the least he could do.

AND NOW, twenty years since, nearing fifty, he could still not shake the sense of shame, that the men in her life had let her down badly. The father who died too young, the husband who murdered her, even the embalmer who could only treat her viscera with cavity fluid, inject her arms and legs and head, stitch the horrible incisions of the postmortem – from left shoulder to breastbone, breastbone to right shoulder, then breastbone to pubic bone – the little bulge in her tummy where the bag full of organs made her look almost expectant, then cover the stitches with cotton and adhesive. And then put a little blush on her cheeks, brush her lipstick on, curl and comb her hair. He had dressed her in the sweater and jeans her mother brought in and lifted her into the casket, put her First Communion rosary in her hand, a crucifix in the head panel of the casket, and put an arm around her mother when she came to look.

'Oh no, no, no', she sobbed, her shoulders rising and falling, her head shaking, her body buckling at the sight of her daughter's dead body. Martin held her at the elbows, whispering, 'Let it go, I'm so sorry', because he never could think of the right thing to say.

Over time Martin learned to live with the helplessness and the sadness and the shame. He quit trying to figure the right thing to say. He listened. He stayed.

Still, all these years since, whenever the right shade of red turned up, he could see the fat old pathologist and his cigar and stupid tutorial manner there in the morgue with its cold smell of disaster and formalin, and the hearse that he drove up to get her that October. And the way they lay in coolers in the corner of the room, the two bodies in trays beside one another – Elena and the son-of-a-bitch that shot her.

He had shot himself, after killing her. He walked back in the house, sat on the edge of the bed, and taking the muzzle of the rifle in his teeth, pulled the trigger with his thumb, dividing his face at the septum in the process.

'Isn't that always the way?' the old pathologist had said, yanking the tray out with Elena's body on it. 'It's lovesickness. A man kills his wife, then kills himself. A woman kills her man, then does her nails.'

Martin hated those sentences and couldn't forget them. That they rang true sometimes and false at others had never been a comfort.

EVENTUALLY, AFTER the wake and Mass, her body was buried beside her father's, leaving another grave on the other side for her mother. It was all Martin could do – to get her where she was supposed to be. Her mother had a stone cut that read

Beloved Daughter with a rose between her dates and another with her own name on it and her year of birth and a dash and had it placed over the open grave beside her husband. She moved away some few years after that. Martin never heard from her again.

Hunter's Moon

SOME DAYS on his walk Harold Keehn thought about his wives. Some days it was caskets. Others it was the heartbreaking beauty of the natural world such as he had come to know it. Often as not the consolidation of these topics was seamless and the names and particulars would race through his brain like a litany in code that only he could decipher. *Elizabeth, goldfinch, Primrose Maple, hemlock, Helen, Mandarin Bronze, osprey, glacier, 18-gauge Perma-Seal, Autumn Oak, chickadee, trillium, Joan.* The list always ended with Joan, his third wife, whom he'd buried last April in a Clarksville Princess Mahogany with a tufted dusty rose velvet interior, in Mullett Lake Cemetery between two blue spruce saplings he'd planted there. The naming gave him a sense of mastery, as if he'd had some say in all of it.

When she had died in early January her body was kept in the cemetery's stone winter vault, waiting for the frost's hold on the ground to give way in the spring and the grave to be opened.

'We don't dig much after the deer season opens', is what Harley Flick, the local sexton, told him, when the graves were arranged for last November, when Harold knew the end was near.

When the racing of names got out of hand Harold would stare intently at the path in front of him, count the cadence of his footfall or breathing and pray for his mind to go blank and hush. Then he could hear the air in the leaves, the lapping of water, the brisk movement of wildlife in the undergrowth. He could imagine the larval stages of next year's hatch of dragon-flies and hexagenia, caddis and stoneflies, the imperceptible growth of antlers and turtle shells, the long pilgrimage of hatchling and fingerling, the return of the grayling and wol-verine. He would try and sense his body's oneness with the pace and nature of the world around him. Better not to think too much, he often thought.

He thought it unlikely he'd ever marry again.

HE DID three or four miles a day, along the abandoned railroad bed through the woods, between his place on the south-west corner of the lake and the village to the north; or south along the west edge of the river mouth, circling the wetlands, where carp spawned in late May and early June, under the interstate and up to the highway, then back again. Some days he'd do more if the weather was fine and his knees didn't ache, or the sciatica hadn't hobbled him, and he was glad for the time out of the house where he found the days, though shortening now, impossibly long. On the best of days he could imagine himself walking all the way to Cheboygan, out on the Straits Highway at the north end of town, along the edge of the big water to Mackinaw City, over the bridge to the Upper Peninsula and into whatever oblivion God had in mind for him. Maybe to Munising or Seney or Manistique – he loved the sound of northern names. And the names of tribes that had named those places: Algonquin and Huron and Chippewa. Or walking south all the way down the mitten of Michigan along the old railway lines through Gaylord and Grayling, Saginaw and Bay City, all the way to Rochester where the tracks passed alongside the house he'd lived in years ago with his first wife before the names of things made much difference to him.

Time occupied for him a kind of geography, the north of which he thought of as the future and the south of which he thought of as the past and where he was at any given moment was the immediate present tense of his personal history, the known point on the map of what he'd call his life and times. It kept him from feeling entirely lost. Some days the future was west and the past east and the moment was shooting craps out in Vegas or some other fantasy, but it always suited him best to think of the whole miserable business as linear. The prospect of time bringing him back around to the point he set forth from was a crueler joke than he could imagine, though the faces of clocks, the evidence of the sun and moon, the repetition of themes in his own life were, of course, disquieting. *Today is a gift*, the sign outside the Topinabee Church read this morning when he'd gone for his oats at the Noka Café. *That's why they call it the present!* Better than last week's bromide, Harold thought: *Fresh spirits have no expiration date!*

Harold stood on his porch, stretching both arms to reach the ceiling, then he dropped his sweatpants and pissed in the general direction of the neighbors' place. Everyone was gone this time of year, back to their jobs and schools and schedules. There were some color tourists and weekenders, but mostly he had the place to himself. He spread his legs, bent at the waist, touched his palms to the ground, feeling the back of his thighs stretch, having to bend his knees ever so slightly now. Then he stood up straight and stretched his arms up over his head again, easing the standing pain in his lower back and right buttock. Then he hitched up his pants, did a couple of slow squats to loosen his knees and side-to-sides to ease the tightness in his groin, and stepped off the porch, pursing his lips to suck in the air. The decadent smell of leaf-fall, the crunch of his footfall in the road's top gravel, the sparkling light of the advancing afternoon, the sweet crispness in the cooling air, the sore pads of his feet, the ringing in his ears – these were all familiar.

If he was hungry after his walk, he told himself, he'd drive into Topinabee for a slab of whitefish or a burger at the Noka. That might kill the time left until nightfall. Once it was dark he could fall asleep watching some cable news or old reruns. Always good to have a plan.

He could hear the dog barking in the distance – Larry Ordway's bat-faced mongrel bitch – frenzied and barking at God knows what. Harold looked along the roadside for a proper stick.

IF HE'D remained married to Elizabeth, today would be their anniversary. Was it forty years yet? He'd lost count. October 29 – the day the stock market crashed and the Great Depression got under way. The day, he'd heard on the radio this morning, the National Organization for Women was founded, the day he was married for the first time, that late October during Vietnam. That figures, he thought, thinking how Elizabeth had left him broke, depressed, vanquished, and confused about women, suffering a kind of post-traumatic stress.

She had left him for a woman.

It all seemed a bit of a blur to him now, and feeling the nerve ends in his right leg warm to the pace he was keeping up Grace Beach Road, he was glad for nature's forgetfulness, how the pain in his ass could be dulled some and the numbness in his legs could be walked out. The afternoon light angling through the woods, the blue sky, the bird noise in the trees, the air rushing in and out of him: life as he knew it, here in the moment, in the gift of the present such as it was, was nothing but a walk in the woods of northern lower Michigan, in mid-autumn.

They'd had a ranch house on three acres in one of the best suburbs north of Detroit. He was a sales rep for Clarksville Casket. All of Michigan – over four hundred funeral homes – was his territory. They had a daughter, Angela, a dog, Maggie, a rosy future. And even if he'd married Elizabeth because he thought marriage was sensible and inevitable, and because he figured as well her as any other; even if he found her, while very attractive, not entirely admirable, even if she had married him to get out of her crazy mother's house, even if they both woke some mornings wondering if they each might have done better for themselves, they had assembled a life. If he had not loved her completely, utterly, irretrievably, he thought then and he thought now, coming to the intersection of Grace Beach and Grandview Beach Roads, he had loved her sufficiently.

Larry Ordway's dog was in full fury now, the sharp blasts of its barking amplified by the general silence in the rest of the world through which Harold's approaching footfall in the gravel was all the more discernible. Harold's grip on the stick tightened in anticipation of the dog's charge down the driveway in real or feigned attack. One never knew what to expect of the bitch. He wanted to be ready for all contingencies. From half a mile off, the dog's distemper sounded menacing. Maybe a raccoon trapped, or skunk or deer, or some late-season cottager going by on a bike or on foot. The dog was a pest – another in a line of disagreeable mixed breeds that had guarded Ordway's empire over the years. It was an empire of sheds and outbuildings, scrap vehicles and rusting implements surrounding his double-wide in the woods at the side of the abandoned railroad easement. The current mutt kept sentry at the top of a long drive that gave onto the road where it curved to cross the tracks. It would come snarling and barking down the drive, chasing off everything that came into its view.

ANGELA, THEIR daughter, was lovely and bright; their lives seemed full of possibilities. They had a manageable mortgage, good credit, good friends, made love twice a week, belonged to the local Congregational church where Elizabeth sang in the choir and was known for a casserole she brought to funeral luncheons and potlucks. Harold ushered for Sunday services. They were the happy young couple with the pretty child.

When Elizabeth turned thirty she went back to school to finish the degree she'd abandoned when she got pregnant. Angela went to day care. Elizabeth commuted to the university and took classes in English and Women's Studies.

Harold was gone a part of most weeks, working his way up and around the state, calling on northern and western accounts. Other times he worked Detroit and the suburbs.

He'd go as far west as Lansing, as far north as Saginaw, and still be home in time for dinner. He'd check the death notices in the Sunday papers to try to get a sense of who'd be in their offices and when. He'd try to see his best accounts every other month, others once a season, others twice a year, some just at convention and some he'd call or send a card to now and then. Some bought better over lunch, others after a few drinks, some over coffee in their offices. Harold had learned to cultivate his relationships with the primary buyers – most often the owner or the owner's son. He'd listen to whatever he had to listen to – their theories on why one unit sold and another didn't, their bad-mouthing of the competition, worries over the crema-tion trend, stories of the latest strange cases: double suicides, remarkably obese cases, multiple fatalities at industrial sites or on the interstates, anything. One week he'd work the city among the ethnic firms – Poles and Romanians, blacks and Jews – then the cushy suburbs of Grosse Point and Bloomfield Hills, up through Pontiac to Flint. Another week he'd work the firms in tri-cities and all the small farm towns in between, spending as much time with the Woolevers in Midland and Cases in Saginaw and Penziens and Stapishes in Bay City with their multiple rooftops and hundreds of calls as the Struthers firm in Reese who did forty funerals a year, but all of them copper or bronze or premium hardwood, paid for in cash by old German farmers. Then he'd take a run out through Ypsi-lanti and Ann Arbor and Jackson along I-94 to Kalamazoo and Grand Rapids, then up to Muskegon and up the west side of the state through the rich resort towns, Traverse City and Charlevoix, Petoskey and Harbor Springs. Once in the spring and once in the fall he'd try to make it through the UP. He'd buy drinks for his accounts at their district meetings and their yearly golf outings and pop for lunches and dinners with his best accounts. He loved the long hours alone in the car and the vacant landscape and the open roads. He'd been through the CB radio craze – his handle was 'Boxman' – and car phones and cell phones, all the gadgets. The drive along Route 2 to the west, then north to Seney, then up to Munising, then west to Marquette was a favorite drive. His accounts up there ordered caskets by the truckload and were accustomed to infrequent deliveries. They'd back up their best units in basements and garages and keep six months' worth of inventory on hand and borrow from their colleagues in the next county if they ran short of a particular unit. And the drive along the east side up the Lake Huron shore from Pinconning and Standish where he'd always lunch at Wheelers for the way it hadn't changed over the years, still serving malted milkshakes in big silver tins and burgers with fried onions and real French fries. Then through Au Gres and Oscoda, Greenbush and Harrisville, all the way up to Alpena and Rogers City along the long blue edge of the state. He'd listen to radio preachers or farm stations that gave the price of sugar beets and alfalfa. Or Paul Harvey or Rush Limbaugh or public radio – it hardly mattered. He called on every firm in every town, promising each to keep their 'line' of Clarksvilles 'exclusive' to prevent comparison shopping between competing firms. If one bought a Tuscany 20-gauge, with lilac crepe for little old ladies, he'd sell the other firm a Silver Rose with pink velvet. If one took the Pietà or Last Supper, the other was pitched the Praying Hands or Old Rugged Cross. He kept sales charts on them all and pushed them to beat last year's averages, convincing them that the more they spent on caskets, the greater return they'd eventually realize on their 'investments.' He left stacks of notepads, pens, and packets of breath mints, each with Clarksville's logo and his contact particulars imprinted. He gave his best accounts custom-made coffee mugs and playing cards with their firm's name embossed next to *Clarksville & Keehn – A Winning Team!*

Elizabeth hadn't exactly left him. She'd put him out. She kept the house, their daughter, the newer of their two cars, and showed him the door.

'You're welcome to stay if you want to,' she told him, 'but I'm sleeping from now on with Eleanor.'

It happened so fast it was a blur to him now. He'd gone from the more or less happy paterfamilias to a man living at loose ends. They'd been married twelve years and it was over in months. Or maybe he was only the last one to know. Either way, he found himself paying the mortgage on a house he no longer lived in, payments on a car he no longer drove, and support for a daughter, now ten years old, he saw all too rarely. That he was paying alimony to a woman with whom he no longer slept vexed him especially at the time. His consortium had been replaced by Dr. Eleanor Dillingham, who taught a course in American Women Poets at the community college.

'Poetry,' she had been quoted as saying, 'like suicide, is something more women attempt and more men accomplish. It is time we changed all that!' The required reading for the course was a book about a madwoman who lived in someone's attic and began, 'Is a pen a metaphorical penis?'

The thought of Dr. Dillingham making love to Elizabeth both excited and disturbed Harold. He could understand their attraction to each other and wondered at the time why they couldn't include him. He found Eleanor oddly fetching himself. He moved out the first weekend in December that year.

One of his accounts gave him the use of rooms over the funeral home garage where he could put a phone and sleep when he wasn't on the road. He took night calls and helped with the removals in trade. A grieving family gathered around the deathbed of a loved and lamented head of the household sent twinges of regret and anger through Harold, but the face he showed to mourners was commiseration. With no particular home to return to, his trips got longer and longer. His sales began to increase as he spent more and more time on the road. Money began to roll in again. He opened an account for his daughter's college fund. He wanted her to go to Alma College, a Presbyterian school in the middle of the state, where he called on the Dewey Funeral Home. The male students there all looked like Young Republicans. Or Albion, where there were mostly Methodists and they didn't teach Women's Studies. Or maybe Calvin College, where modest Dutch Reform girls and boys were monitored for proper conduct.

Come Fridays he'd stay on wherever he was. He'd take a room in Grand Rapids or Ishpeming or Port Huron. He'd coax his last account out for a boozy dinner and offer to help out with the Saturday funerals and sit in the motel watching TV or in the lounge listening to the terrible music and hoping to get lucky with one of the local women.

He bought the house on the lake the year after the divorce. He'd heard about it from the account in Indian River who had buried the widow who had lived in it for years. It was old and a little ramshackle but it had a good foundation and two hundred feet of frontage and could be bought right from the old woman's children, who lived in Ohio.

Harold saw in it a refuge from the rootlessness he felt – a place to bring his daughter for those summer vacations and winter breaks his visitation rights entitled him to. He envisaged her long into the rosy future, learning to fish and ski and name the species of things with him, then perhaps bringing a boyfriend up for the weekend. He saw her wedding on the lawn under a great tent on a blue day in July or August, and his eventual grandchildren gathered round the barbecue for family reunions, playing badminton or horseshoes, or paddling canoes out on the sparkling water, all housed in the dormer he would in due course build over the big garage – everyone together, all distance and divisions healed. He saw, however dimly, all of them circling his last illness, or bearing him to some proper disposition, then returning to the family home on the lake to toast his life and times and memory – a man, they would say, who had played the cards life dealt him, and played them well, and would be sorely missed.

Quality time, he told himself; less is more, if better spent.

It had a stone fireplace in the main room and a good well and a wide front porch and a screened porch off the front bedroom upstairs from which he could watch the lake and the stars and the northern lights. The sunrise poured into the windows; he slept to the lapping of lake water. He compensated for fewer visits downstate by inviting his accounts up for a weekend's fishing or snowmobiling or hunting or cards. He'd take them to the Breakers Bar in Topinabee, get them a little liquored up, buy them a steak, pitch the latest additions to the line, and take their orders. He'd write off the expenses on his tax returns. His market share kept getting better and better. His up-line in Indiana were all full of praise. There was talk of a job at headquarters, maybe something salaried in marketing.

The business was all about 'protection' then. Just like diamonds and deodorants, tampons and defense budgets, caskets were sold on the Cold War notion that they could be 'sealed' and 'safe' and would 'protect' the body more or less 'forever' from leakage or embarrassment or unforeseen dangers. It was the marketing theme. Harold would spend hours extolling the virtues of Clarksville's gum-rubber gaskets, 'cathodic protection' — a magnesium bar than ran down the bottom of their heavier-gauge steels which was said to retard rust — and the 48-ounce Solid Copper Omega which 'grew stronger through age by oxidation.' 'Precious metals', he called the bronze and the copper units. 'Permanent protection.' The more product knowledge his accounts had, the more product they'd buy and the more they'd sell and the better he'd do.

The second summer after he and Elizabeth divorced, Angela came up to the lake and stayed with him for a couple of weeks. She was just on the brink of becoming a teen. Harold could sense the changes coming. He resolved to have her bedroom redecorated when she'd come up next year 'for the whole summer.' But after he married Helen, she first demurred — a conflict with summer volleyball — and then refused. Angela said that her mother said that her father was an incurable heterosexual, bound to dominate women, a member of the patriarchy, a serial rapist, and a hopeless case. Angela told him all of this in a letter Harold figured her mother typed. She was turning thirteen. Elizabeth's anger at his remarriage was something he never understood. That she passed it along to Angela was even more inexplicable. Harold called often but Angela was always 'out'. He sent flowers for her birthday. He sent her cards and letters she never responded to. It hurt him, but he blamed it on her mother. He tried to stay in touch but figured he was best off leaving her alone. She had enough to deal with, with all the changes in her little life. He didn't want to pull her into a conflict. He thought the day would come when she was older, that she would understand her father better and they could reestablish a relationship. It never happened.

When she was sixteen, Angela was hit by a train. She'd been walking the tracks that ran between Main Street and the Mill Pond early on a Sunday morning. The autopsy showed that she'd been drinking and was pregnant. And though the death was ruled accidental, Harold wondered if she might have thrown herself in front of the train, and if so, which of her parents should be blamed. It also occurred to him that maybe the man who had impregnated her pushed her in front of the train. He wondered if it was a man or a boy. Had she been looking for another father figure in her life or just playing around with one of the pimply jerk-offs she'd grown up with. Knowing the cause of death while not knowing the cause of the cause of death sent Harold into a spiral of such steep descent that he resolved to put it all out of his mind, void as that darkness was of any place names he could recognize; he feared the point of no return.

Elizabeth arranged to have Angela's body cremated, to which Harold agreed, but he insisted on putting her in a Melrose Cherry instead of the cardboard casket they always used when there wasn't going to be a public viewing. 'A shame to burn such a beautiful piece of wood', Elizabeth had said, when they went to the funeral home to identify their daughter's body. She rubbed her hand along the deeply polished finish, averting her eyes from the body in the box. He wanted to hit her. He wanted to put his fist through her face and shut her mouth forever. But he only nodded and thought, Yes, a shame.

Angela's face was unmarked, all the injuries apparently 'internal'. He and Elizabeth divided the ashes. Each got a little cherub-shaped urn with half their daughter's remains inside.

He never knew what his former spouse had done with her half of their daughter. He never asked. He hadn't spoken to Elizabeth since.

HAROLD DIDN'T know Larry Ordway, or even if Larry was his name. It might have been Lenny or Louie or Lester. All the sign said was *L. Ordway Private*, scrawled on a white board in blue paint and nailed to a tree stump at the end of the drive. Harold couldn't remember when he settled on Larry or why exactly, or how he'd come to several conclusions about a man he had never met. There was the cross that went up in the woods one year, painted white and gold and ten feet tall and wired for lights, big bulbs, that shone through the dark eerily – a sign of the born-again Christian fundamentalist, Michigan militia type of head case he reckoned Larry Ordway must be. And there were the mean-spirited dogs always challenging him at the bend in the road, barking, baring their teeth, the current one now five or six years into its miserable life, looking like the hound of hell with its frothing muzzle and pointed ears. Harold had feared it and picked up his pace to get past its purview and kept an eye out even when he was out of range. He had taken long detours through the woods to keep out of the dog's way, his fear getting the best of him until once, the week after Joan had been diagnosed, Harold had waited for the dog, growled back at it as it hunched and snarled, and taunted it with waving arms and timed it perfectly so that when the cur lunged within kicking range, he caught it squarely in its yapping mouth, a perfect punt, flipping it on its backside and sending it yelping back up the drive. It hadn't really challenged Harold since. Its barking was vicious but still it kept its cowering distance. Harold kept a stick handy just in case, half hoping it would give him another go. Sometimes now, after he'd gotten past Ordway's, he'd hear movement in the dense woods on either side of the railway easement, aside and behind him, and wondered if the dog was following along, waiting to pounce or wanting to make friendly. Harold didn't know but didn't trust the thing. He'd turn sometimes and look behind him. Once or twice he thought he caught a glimpse of the bitch crossing the tracks in a blur, maybe stalking him, waiting for its chance to settle the score.

At Hobo Beach, where the trail ran nearest the lake, Harold stopped to sit and watch the water for one of the eagles that nested nearby or the osprey that nested on a platform placed in the river mouth by the DNR, or anything else that might happen. The rapturous descent of fishing birds, the haunted call of loons, the hovering of kingfishers, the uncommon beauty of common mergansers – these incarnations now remembered, late in the day, late in the year, made him feel a fortunate pilgrim indeed. Above the treeline on the far side of the lake the fat face of the full moon was emerging. Harvest moon, he thought. No, hunter's moon, then beaver moon, then cold. He ran through the names of moons such as he knew them. There would be moon shadows tonight and light on the water.

All the docks and boat hoists were stacked on the beach, waiting for the coming winter's freeze and deep snows and next spring's thaw – worm moon, he thought in March, pink moon April, May, the flower moon – before being hauled out and reassembled in the water for the high season. The boaters and sunbathers all gone south and the snowmobiles not yet thinking about coming north, the off-season vacancy of late October struck Harold as the best of all times of year.

This golden harvest aspect of it all, a feast for all souls, the sense of finished work and jobs done well – 'Autumn Oak' is what he named the clear-finished, hand-polished number with the fallen-leaf appliqué stitched into the cap panel and the tailored beige linen interior when he first beheld it, and his bosses at Clarksville had agreed with him. They even designed an urn to go with it – same wood, same finish, same falling leaves machine-etched into it – a package deal for the cremation crowd. 'The Autumn Oak Ensemble', they called it in the catalogue, and sold them by the truckload all over the place – the most popular of Clarksville's hardwood line.

HE SHOULD have been better to Helen. She had never been anything but good to him. Maybe if he'd been more trusting, less damaged goods, not so angry. Maybe if Angela had lived. He didn't know. He often wished he could do that over again, make it up to her.

They'd met at the convention in Grand Rapids. Her booth for Barber Music Systems was next to Clarksville's on the exhibit floor. By the last day of the convention he worked up the nerve to ask her to dinner. She was younger, plain-faced, smarter and more pleasant than anyone he'd been out with in years. Her father had started the business, which sold background music systems for mortuaries – hours of hymns or new age music to 'Break the Terrible Silence of Grief'. Under Helen's guidance the company was marketing video memorial tributes.

They dated for six months, then got engaged, then got married. They honeymooned at Casa de Campo in the Dominican Republic. He golfed, she sunbathed. It was good but brief. They divorced soon after Angela's death. Helen had the marriage annulled and was soon enough remarried to a man from Forethought Preneed who didn't drink as Harold had begun to and didn't sleep around, the way Harold did in the months following his daughter's death. Helen wasn't bitter. She just wanted out. She wished him well, but wouldn't hang around for his 'self-destruction'.

He saw her at conventions after that. She'd always smile sweetly and keep her distance. He'd readied the little speech to make amends and ask forgiveness, to say it had all been his fault and bad timing and the drink, of course, but when he approached her in her booth the year before he retired, her eyes looked panicky, she put one hand over her mouth and the other out straight as if to warn him off. 'I'm sorry,' he said, 'I just wanted to say . . .' but she looked frightened and her eyes were filling with tears and she was backing away as if from some peril or contagion, so he stopped and turned away and said nothing. He thought maybe he'd write it all in a letter, to let her know he knew how bad he'd been to her. But he never got around to it and thought now, sitting by the lake, watching the moon rise, that he likely never would.

He stood and sighed heavily and stretched and, dropping his pants, pissed in the sand and, after hitching up again, walked back from the water's edge to the trail along the railway bed he'd been on. It was here he'd seen an indigo bunting once, perched on the head of a cattail by the water, a blueness he had never seen before or since. He felt a chill in the evening air. Looking down the long tunnel between the trees, Harold watched for deer crossing, or porcupine, or beaver. He looked back the way he'd come for signs of Larry Ordway's dog. Nothing moved. Once, years back, he had seen what he swore was a black bear pausing in the clearing with its nose in the air. He knew that the woods held red fox and gray wolf, but he had never seen them. Signs of life in the deep interior, seen and unseen, quickened in him the kind of gladness he remembered having as a boy. The emergency flight of pheasant and wild turkey, the passing shadows of osprey and vulture and gull, the trees fed on by nuthatch and pileated woodpecker, felled by beaver, scraped by whitetail bucks, mauled he imagined by bear and raccoon – these apparitions of the world's natural order were a comfort to him for reasons he could not articulate.

It was Harold Keehn who had convinced Clarksville to market wooden caskets, the rich grains, the homey cabinetry warmth of it all. And Harold who came up with the idea of planting trees, saplings only, pennies only by way of expense, in cahoots with the forestry department, for every Clarksville casket sold. The Memory Tree Program had been a huge success. It assuaged the baby boomers' natural concerns about ecology and conservation and renewable resources. He'd pitched the whole market shift at a sales conference in a presentation he called 'Don't Let Your Business Go Up in Smoke' in which he noted the growing popularity of cremation and the natural consumer preference for boxes that would burn. 'Permanence' and 'Protection' had given way to 'Natural Beauty' and 'Sensible Choices'. A woman's right to choose, thought Harold, applied to the recently widowed as well as the recently impregnated, noting the coincident rise in the abortion and cremation rates. 'If you can't beat 'em, join 'em', he told his bosses at Clarksville headquarters. 'Give them plenty of choices'. They called their cremation catalogue *Options by Clarksville* and filled it with urns and cremation caskets.

Had it not been for the drinking and carousing that everyone knew about but no one mentioned, he might have been given a vice presidency, stock options, an office at headquarters in Indiana. As it was they thanked him for his insights and cut his territory. He didn't care. Inflation kept his commissions high. He had nothing to save for. His dead daughter's college fund went into a couple of mutual funds and swelled during the 1990s. He had more than he'd ever need. His place was paid off. After Angela had died, after Helen left, very little mattered until he met Joan at an AA meeting in a church basement in Topinabee.

She had looked to be about the age Angela would have been if she had lived. She always listened to Harold carefully when he talked at the weekly meetings. She nodded and smiled when it came his turn to tell how he was powerless over alcohol and his life had become unmanageable or how he'd come to believe that a power greater than himself could restore him to sanity or the particulars of his searching and fearless moral inventory. She would nod and smile and at the end she would squeeze his hand after the Our Father or the recitation of the Serenity Prayer and give him a hug and tell him, 'Easy does it, Harold.' She was so happy, it seemed, so very happy. And whatever calamity or sadness brought her to AA, details of which she shared frankly on occasion, she seemed to inhabit a permanent present tense, free of the past and future, afloat on the moment she occupied. She was pretty and had a graceful body and eyes like the blue of the indigo bunting he had only seen once. When Harold asked her if he could ask her out to dinner, she said she'd rather bring him dinner at home. It was a chicken and rice casserole, and pecan pie for dessert. She stayed that night and the night after that and on the weekend they moved her out of the rooming house in Cheboygan, her entire estate fitting easily in the trunks of their two cars. There had never been any talk of marriage. They were companions and occasional lovers, generous with each other in ways that were new to Harold. He took her walleye fishing and built fires in the fall and winter. She read to him in bed and cooked him breakfast. He took her on sunset cruises along the lakeshore in an old wooden inboard he bought for such occasions, savoring the changing light and night skies and the silence that would sometimes settle between them. She quit her job at the marina where she did payables and receivables. He did most of his business by phone and fax. They went to dinner in Petoskey and Mackinaw City and Indian River, movies in Gaylord and Cheboygan. She abided his long walks, his long silences, his darker moods. Whenever she touched him, or talked to him, or looked at him, Harold felt alive. And though he never could figure out why she came and stayed – she was twenty-three years younger and might have had a more exciting life – his gratitude was manifest and he treated her accordingly.

He bought a small RV and they would leave just before Memorial Day, driving around the country on no particular schedule, returning after Labor Day when all the summer neighbors had returned to their downstate lives. He kept a list of the place names they had been to. She kept albums full of photos, each of them posing for the other, in front of some diner or park entrance or stop in the road. They had lived together there on the lake for over ten years. The best years of his life, he would always say. The best of hers, she would say in return. Only when her death seemed certain had they agreed to marry so that Harold could be her next of kin. Her family in Lansing was long estranged. None came during her sickness or after she died, though Harold made the requisite phone calls. Whatever happened between her and her family happened years ago, the detachment having achieved a point, apparently, of no return.

Joan's cancer took a year and a half from first diagnosis, to the surgery to remove a lung, through the radiation and chemo and eventual reoccurrence – the 'irregularity' they called it when it showed back up – to the morning last winter when, after an awful seizure, because it had grown into her brain, she died with Harold sitting helplessly by.

After the burial he'd ordered a stone with her name and dates on it – *Joan Winters Keehn* – but he'd never seen it, though he passed the cemetery often enough: he never thought of her as there. But some nights over the past months, he'd go out in the motor home and sit at the table where they'd play gin rummy nights on the road; or he'd crawl into the bed where they had slept in their summer travels, pressed to one another, his right hand cupping her small left breast in their genial embrace. Some nights alone out there in the RV in the driveway, he'd wonder if it was time to take up drink again. So far he hadn't on the advice that Joan herself had always given out, that there was no sadness that couldn't be made more miserable by the addition of a Class A depressant. Still, the brand names of whiskeys were beginning to make their way onto the lists of names he kept – Jameson's, Bushmills, Powers, and Paddy – with the names of birds and the names of caskets, the names of moons and towns and tribes and names of his lost wives.

Harold Keehn could imagine Adam in the garden, that first index finger working overtime, assigning to every new thing he saw, fresh, orderly syllables – aardvark, apple, elephant, waterfall – as if to name it was to know it or own it or anyway to have, if not dominion over it, some consortium with it. He wondered how it must have been when that first man first whispered 'Eve' and the woman turned to look into his eyes.

When Harold found himself at the south edge of Topinabee, the hum of the highway coming through the woods on his left and the moon on the water on his right, he knew he'd walked too far. How had he lost track of it all? And turning back to go the way he'd come, he wondered if there would be enough light left in the day for the way home. Even at his best pace it would take him nearly an hour. Suddenly he was aware of his body and its pains and aches. His knee was grinding, his feet aflame, the small of his back full of crippling twinges. He was fatigued. The air was getting colder now and the wind off the lake increasing. He resolved to keep, in spite of everything, a steady pace.

He'd quit the casket trade at the right time, Harold thought. It was no longer the permanence and protection of the metal ones, or the warmth and natural attractions of the woods. Now it was all gimmicks and knickknacks. Interchangeable corner hardware – tackle boxes for fishermen, plastic mum plants for gardeners, little faux carrots and kitchen utensils for women who cooked, all molded in plastic – How silly, he thought. And 'memory drawers' – the little box-within-the-box to put farewell notes and mementos in – smarmy malarkey thought up by 'focus groups' and test markets. Back in his day it was the salesman on his rounds who came back with the best ideas. What the public wanted in a casket, Harold had told the honchos at home office, was a way to 'get a handle' on it all – a death in the family – the once-in-a-lifetime aspect of it all. Trouble was it was the ultimate one-to-a-customer deal. And hard enough to get folks enthused about even the one.

Now he was aware of the angling lights that lit the way before him. The golden rays of evening washing through the trees on his right and the silver of the moonrise over the lake on his left illumined the track of railway bed before him. It took his breath away, the beauty of it. His chest was heavy. He sighed.

When Joan's Princess Mahogany was moved last April, from the stone winter vault to the freshly opened grave, the seams of the boards in the casket lid were splitting where the epoxy had dried in the cold interior of the holding tomb. Condensation, desiccation, extremes in freeze and thaw: Even the best of boxes will eventually rot, he thought. Everything in nature disappears. Harley Flick let Harold bury his daughter's ashes, the half that he had kept in the house these many years, in the room she never came to stay in, in the same new grave as Joan was buried in. He poured his daughter's ashes over his third wife's casket where they filled in the open seams in the lid. Then he borrowed Harley's shovel and filled half the muddy grave himself before Harley finished the job with his John Deere backhoe.

When Harold turned off the rail easement by Larry Ordway's cross, the dog lay dozing in the road at the bottom of the drive and hardly budged when Harold walked by. He'd let his stick go miles back. Turning down Grace Beach Road, on the last leg of the journey, he looked back and saw the dark shape of the dog behind him. It was not barking or bothered or giving chase, just following him at Harold's own pace, silhouetted by the last light of the sun behind it. He was aware of his heart racing and his breath laboring and the general ache of his body sharpening and the fatigue of the long walk overtaking him. If the dog attacked he could not fend him off. But the dog did not attack, only followed Harold home, footsore, winded, aching, spent.

Harold slumped on the bottom step of his front porch, watching the last light pour out of the day and the moonlight widening over the flat surface of water and the darkness tightening all around him. He avoided the impulse to name some stars that appeared in the firmament, or to name some fish swimming unseen in the dark waters, or whatever living things moved in the woods. He wouldn't be going to Topinabee. He didn't want a drink. He wouldn't build a fire tonight. In his flesh he felt entirely quenched. It was enough to let his vision blur watching the water and the moon and to find Larry Ordway's dog, if Larry was Ordway's name at all, curled beside him free of menace, watching nothing happen, thinking nothing of substance, void of memory or purpose or expectation. Neither the names of breeds nor the names of dogs nor the names of their owners troubled him anymore. The dog kept watch all night and did not howl at the rising or the falling moon.

Matinée de Septembre

AISLING PREFERRED FRENCH press coffee, pinhead oatmeal, cymbidium orchids, and Mahler adagiettos. She
loved the tiny courtesies – the door held open, hand-
written thank-you notes, engraved invitations, a man who rose
when she left the table – a thing Nigel had always done. She
found an attention to detail assuring: the pilots' crisp epaulets,
the fashionable scarves of the stewardesses. The way Delibes'
Flower Duet was played during the boarding process, to calm
the possibly anxious passengers, the little packet with the tooth-
paste and toothbrush and blindfold and booties, the blanket
wrapped in plastic, the headphones, the manifest efficiency of
the cabin crew dispensing preflight orange juices, their starched
white cotton shirts and blouses. British Airways seemed, like
all things British, more civilized somehow than the American
carriers. Aisling wondered if her sense of it was defensible.

She settled into seat 51H of the nethermost World Traveller

section of the plane with the certain knowledge that even here, in steerage, she would be treated with the same dignity as the balding men and their trophy wives already on their second cocktails in first class, with their personal TVs and cushy quarters.

Bigger seats for bigger asses, is what she thought, a little startled by her sudden hostility but pleased to think that they had to pay so much more for the same time in the air, the same travel, more or less the same amenities. Oh, they might get better movies, real silverware, more legroom, and, of course, first on, first off boarding and deplaning privileges. But at the end of the day they would still be asses – big, fat, balding asses whose wives only traveled with them for the shopping ops, the change of scenery, and the chance of meeting someone really interesting. She rubbed her right temple where a headache was forming. Aisling could identify in herself more sudden shifts in temper lately and a low-grade, ever-present contempt for white males past a certain age – older men with money and position, confidence and self possession. Was it age or the early onset of something? Perhaps a product of her education – postfeminist, postmodern. That she had been briefly married to a man of this description; that she was the daughter of just such a man – these were among the exceptions that proved the rule. No need for the perfect to upbraid the good, she told herself. Even if asses, men could be of use.

Aisling was privately pleased with the size of her own ass, its shape and contour, tiny really for a woman at forty and still very firm. An occasionally vegetarian youth, a whole-foods adult-hood, the eschewing of red meats in favor of fish, the odd bit of free-range chicken, no sugars or breads or potatoes, plenty of greens and roughage, brown rice, and regular exercise – jogging

as a girl, long walks as a woman – neither the sedentary habits
of an academic life, the shape-shifting perils of pregnancy, nor
the occasional binges of chocolate and cheeses or some finer
wine; and yes, she would have to confess, every now and then
a Big Mac and fries, just for the decadence of it. No conspiracy
of age or maternity or indulgence had added more than a dozen
pounds in two dozen years to the body she had as a girl of sixteen. 'A small package', is what Nigel had called her during their
courtship, when he couldn't get enough of her. 'A small package
in a large world', he would whisper in the voice he had wooed her
in. There had been a lovely imbalance to their lovemaking. He
was always so grateful, so full of praise, naming her specific parts
and his reverence for them. It was his age. They'd married when
she wasn't yet thirty and he was just gone sixty. She'd been his
student, then his assistant, then his lover, then his wife, then his
widow. Now she was his bibliographer and minder of his reputation. She had his letters and notebooks, his unpublished poems
and variorums. And, though her thick black hair was graying,
though her dark brown eyes appeared too often tired, and she
read with bifocals now, she remained a woman with good skin,
a girlish figure in which she took, seeing so many women of
her age gone bulky, a secret pride and quiet pleasure. Age was
irreversible. But if she was not voluptuous as a girl, she neither
sagged as a woman. If her breasts were small – 'fried eggs' her
father called them, inappropriately, in her teens – they defied
now the pendulous gravity of larger, fleshier, fatter bodies. She
had, despite the baby and her age, the bosom of a woman much
younger. She looked good in no bra or a Wonderbra, pantsuits
or little black dresses, vintage lingerie or plaid pajamas. And she
knew men noticed her, and that her figure quickened in them,
if not desire, then admiration, even appreciation.

She sat up straight in 51H, tucked the pillow and the blanket on one side of her, the canvas bag with her American publisher's logo on it, full of magazines, hand cream, bottled water, and travel essentials on the other side of her. She still had plenty of room for comfort – a small package, flying steerage from London to Detroit on British Airways Flight 202 on the last leg of six weeks of literary duties – a professor and poet of note, a person of substance and discernment, trusted and tenured, who though seated in the back of the plane was nonetheless flying on someone else's dime. She prayed for a vacant spot between her and the red-haired woman, twenty years her senior, applying her makeup in the window seat.

She could have flown as easily in the front as in the back. Money was never the issue with her. She was – though few of her colleagues or students knew it – the daughter of one of Detroit's first families. Her father had made a fortune in auto parts and owned a share of one of the professional sports teams. He'd established a trust fund in Aisling's name before she'd started grade school. She'd had access to it since she was twenty-one. She could have drawn on those resources, or on the not-inconsiderable accounts of her late husband. She'd recently sold some of his papers to the university archivist for enough to remodel their bungalow in Burns Park – one of Ann Arbor's respectable neighborhoods. It had more advanced degrees per capita than even the wealthier exurbs. And she was as well paid as anyone on the English faculty. Still, both the front of the bus and the back had their special privileges and the idea that she traveled for free was more appealing than the idea that she traveled in style.

She watched as other passengers boarded the plane and for a moment wondered if these might be the people she'd be dying with. Might some malfunction or shoe bomber or flock of seabirds bring the plane down over the Atlantic? Or some small outpost in Scotland – everyone blown to bits in the carnage? The whiff of disaster and mortality was agitating and she searched in her purse for her medication and something a colleague had given her for airsickness. She pressed on the point of the pain in her temple, rubbed her eyes. She wondered if she could get a drink.

She smiled at the cabin steward, a young Indian or Pakistani, passing out pamphlets. He was so pretty. Olive-skinned, dark-eyed, twenty-something, slightly built but muscular. His crisp white short-sleeved shirt with the epaulets, the blue tie. He must be gay, she thought. 'The best ones always are. Then she scolded herself for thinking such thoughts – right out of a sitcom or chick flick. But they *are!* she thought, and scolded herself again. She could see that he paid attention to his body hair and the press of his trousers. But if he weren't, she wondered, which of her parts would his hands first go to – breasts or cheekbone? Buttocks or genitalia? Or might he, as Nigel had, trace the slow curve of her eyebrow with his index finger? She did not scold herself for such thoughts, but regretted nonetheless the absence of answers. She sighed, resigned to the prospect that that part of her life was over.

Aisling read the *Menu and Destination Guide* he'd given her. How very helpful, such a nice touch. Like flying in a café instead of a bus. Dinner would be a choice of 'Southwestern-Style Chicken Breast with Sweet Corn Salsa and Rice' or 'Prosciutto and Ricotta Cheese Lasagna on a Bed of Spinach'. There would be wines and cheeses and a sweet. Detroit's average July/August temperature was 24 degrees centigrade, the booklet helpfully informed. There was a quick conversion guide: C × 2

+ 32 = *F*. Hotter than either Ireland or England had been and nearly twice as much summer rainfall as the British Isles. The packet included a map of Michigan and the city of Detroit and its environs. Familiarity indeed breeds contempt, she thought. She remembered the packet on the flight coming over, six weeks before. How she had savored the shape of the names: *Marylebone, Bloomsbury, Holborn, Strand, Soho, the City,* and *Mayfair* – she loved the contorted streetscape and the wide slice of the Thames through the middle and she had squinted to look at the names of the bridges: *Lambeth, Westminster, Waterloo.* She'd looked at the space between Theobalds Road and Guilford Street, bordered on the west by Southampton Row and, on the east, by Gray's Inn Road, in Holborn, where her friend Vanessa lived in Orde Hall Street and where she'd stayed while in London before she and Vanessa took the train from Paddington to Exeter for their duties in Devon. It was Vanessa who had put her name in for the Arvon Foundation course, as someone who would make an excellent co-tutor.

Vanessa had been to Ann Arbor the year before to do a reading and to lecture on Modern British Poets. Aisling had liked her immediately, her poems, her no-nonsense style in workshops and lectures, and her rich midlife sexuality. 'Why is it', she had asked Aisling at the reception following her triumphant reading in the Rackham Amphitheater, 'visiting male poets get offers of sex from the graduate students, and visiting women get unsolicited manuscripts?' There'd been a little scandalous buzz about Vanessa and one of the first-year M.F.A. fictionists with whom she had left the reception, arm in arm.

Aisling had invited her to lunch the next day. They had traded books, email addresses, gossip about other poets. They had stayed in touch.

Once the Arvon Foundation had invited Aisling to England, it was easy enough to find other programs willing to host her. She'd read and presented a paper at the Yeats Summer School, lectured at Queens and Cheltenham.

Her colleagues at the university, stuck with their lackluster summer stints at literary summer camps and writers' colonies, could not fail to be impressed by Aisling's summer duties in the British Isles. She had sent them postcards of Totleigh Barton – a two-story manse from the twelfth century covered with thatch, surrounded by outbuildings and the green Devon countryside or of Yeats's grave at Drumcliff, or of Pre-Raphaelites from the Tate Gallery.

In Aisling's department at the university, most of the men angled for Bread Loaf in Vermont, famous for its flings, or maybe a stint at Yaddo or MacDowell Colony or Sewanee, or a summer term at a nicely situated private college. Only the elders in her department expected to cross the Atlantic on the strength of their work. Some, of course, had been to European conferences in their specialties – Renaissance Writers or Women's Studies or Translations of Modern Russian Writers. But they were scholars on scholarly business – may as well, thought Aisling, have been bankers or ophthalmologists. Aisling traveled as artist and academic, poet and scholar, maker of beauty and witness to it.

Whatever claims to fame her colleagues had, they would have to admit that she had developed an international standing, however modest. Two slim volumes from a respectable university press in America and now the promise of a book on the shelves in Britain and Ireland. She would add it all to the personal page on the faculty website the university maintained.

She had been flown and housed and fed and paid and publicly feted for her time and talents. She had slipped the dull gravity of the everyday schedule and ordinary geography and been borne aloft, by the power of words she had written in private, published in fetching if fairly limited editions, and she was now being returned home from the ancient outposts of the English-speaking world.

'Please fasten your seat belt, madam.'

The pretty Indian or Pakistani was leaning across her, bringing her seat back and tray table to their full upright position. He had one hand on the button on the armrest at her side, the other behind her, moving the headrest forward. She could smell his soap and talcum powder. Something from Harrods or Jermyn Street.

'May I get a drink?'

'We're about to take off.'

'All the more reason', she smiled at him.

'Once we're airborne, I'll be back around, madam.'

Eye candy, Aisling thought to herself, and scolded herself for thinking it. He must be gay. She scolded herself again.

The plane was speeding down the runway. Aisling closed her eyes and wondered if the pills were working. Though she wasn't sure of God anymore, she was praying for safety and deliverance. She did not want to die with these people. The whining children two rows ahead of her, the school soccer team at the head of her section, the redheaded woman applying awful lipstick beside her – what if these were her neighbors in death? She had much more living to do.

Suddenly the thought of returning to university in a couple of weeks, the return to the dull routines of the classroom and committee work, the needs of students and colleagues, the pressures of performance – it was all more than disturbing to her. She was sure it was the source of what was now a splitting headache, the stiffness in her shoulders, a panic taking shape. Whether it was this or the sudden press of mortality that air travel always stirred in her – as the jet raced down the runway toward its takeoff – she resolved to extend her summer travels. She was not yet ready to go home to Burns Park to wait out the remainder of August sweltering in town, preparing syllabuses and lecture notes. No, she would make for someplace without duties or details, social or literary obligations; someplace where she could let herself be pampered and excessive, waited on and catered to, where she could read for pleasure, sleep at all hours, bask in the absence of obligations; where she might restore herself after long travel and hard labor in distant places, before returning to the daily grind of the fall semester. A fortnight of utter self-indulgence, ease, and tranquillity, she thought, just what she needed. This craving for freedom, release, forgetfulness, she would indulge it. She could not only afford it, she thought she could not afford not to do it – the better for her students in the long run, to restore herself before pouring herself out in service of their needs. Better to return to her office in Angell Hall, to the eventual committee meetings and faculty teas, looking as well rested as she was well traveled. The headaches and insomnia that seemed now her ever-present scourges might be mended by two weeks of ease.

So ran her thoughts as the plane climbed upward and outward from its earthbound gravity and the signal sounded that allowed them to unlock their seat belts and move about the cabin. Aisling decided to study the maps in the back of her in-flight magazines and to use the hours of her return flight to decide on a further destination. She was determined to land in Detroit with a location in mind to escape it all again, to spend the last two weeks of August in pursuit of bliss and rejuvenation.

AISLING BLACK was born in Birmingham, an upmarket northern suburb of Detroit, in the year Martin Luther King and Bobby Kennedy were killed and Nixon was elected president. She was the only daughter of a man who made a respectable fortune selling safety glass to Detroit's automakers. Her mother taught elementary school, read Plath and Sexton, and died young of a subarachnoid hemorrhage. Her father never remarried, rather threw himself more deeply into work, finding ways to embed antennae and defrosting elements in the glass, amassing thereby a quite substantial fortune. A dead mother and often absent father produced a brainy, sometimes brooding girl who edited her grade school newspaper, won all the academic prizes in high school, tested well enough to get scholarships to all the better Eastern universities. After an undergraduate degree in Vermont she got her M.F.A. and Ph.D. in California, where she had studied with the famous poet. If she hadn't yet created much in the way of beauty, she nonetheless knew beauty when she saw it. And she had seen in Nigel's long, brutish poems, full of the blood and bone of his father's butcher shop in Seattle, something raw and sensual. He was one of Roethke's last students, had taught with Berryman at Minnesota, quoted Lowell and Bishop and Robert Frost, and was fairly manic, famously bingey, and, Aisling thought, a brilliant teacher. And he was handsome in the way men are who know how to wear the proper jacket and tie, a hat in winter, a cashmere coat; men who could be counted on for

good directions and clean handkerchiefs, even if they sometimes seemed to look too long in the wrong direction or drank
too much or said outrageous things. He could speak in meta-
phors, assigning depth to the everyday, connecting elements
of the tedious and mundane to the stuff of art and literature.
He had praised her poems in his workshop and attended her
reading in the student union. When he invited her to travel
with him, the year between her master's and doctoral studies,
on a cross-country tour to mark the publication of his selected
poems, she accepted. It was out of character for her to do so.
But he made it sound more like a job than an assignation and
an important part of her education. And it was. He was twice
her age and worldly in ways she wanted to learn from. She
started as his companion and personal assistant, someone
whose discipline about travel arrangements and scheduling
allowed him freedom from such drudgeries. He would show
up, the crazy genius, wow the audience with his performance,
sign the books, and say outlandish things that would guarantee coverage in the local press. She would get him to the next
stop in one piece, make all the arrangements for lodging and
meals and local transport. She worked with his publisher to do
press releases, managed the book signings, the radio and print
interviews. Eventually they became lovers. Sex with a man past
his prime was more tuned to the timing of her own body than
the more urgent or furtive lovers she'd been with before. If
his performance was flagging, his desire was intense, and it
aroused her. Everything took longer with Nigel. Talk was an
essential part of the seduction. So was food. His patience was
consummate, his gratitude endearing, his amazement at her
little body, its parts and zones and regions and responses, a
constant blushing. 'Classic beauty on a peasant's form', he said,

lathering her body in the shower. He genuflected and kissed her. She came to love him. They moved in together. She proposed marriage. He agreed.

Theirs had been the perfectly bargained marriage. Each got something in the deal. He wanted her youth and beauty and trust-fund security, no less her scholarly instincts and disciplines – the better to burnish his postmortems. She wanted his age and experience and manic freedom. She wanted access to his generation of writers and poets. He loved her young friends always asking him questions about poets now dead whom he remembered. Both assumed it would not last forever – 'Such habits are not suited to the long haul', he'd said – which made any awkwardness the more bearable.

When she finished her doctorate – her dissertation on the Maud Gonne poems of W. B. Yeats was published by a reputable university press – he gladly agreed to follow her back to Michigan, where she could be nearer her widowed father. The department had made them a 'package' deal to get them to move from California. He was given an endowed chair with the graduate writing program. He had minimal teaching duties, charge over the visiting writers' program, and funds allotted for an annual conference. She was given a fellowship and the promise of a tenure-track position. They bought a house on Granger Avenue in Burns Park with a big backyard and front porch and good kitchen. Their soirees for visiting writers were sources of great gossip among faculty and graduate students and were sometimes reviewed in the *Ann Arbor News*. Nigel knew everyone still alive and assisted the university in attracting the best writers to Ann Arbor. He knew the requirements of visiting poets, the foibles of writers on the road; he was great at introductions and literary intrigues. And he made Aisling his ever-present 'partner in crime', a woman half his own age whose manifest intelligence made her choice to be with him all the more a prize – he loved being seen with her and made no secret of his dependence on her.

His tenderness when her only pregnancy ended after eight months in the stillbirth of a tiny son made her love him unequivocally. He had a stone cut with the infant's name, his own name, and the only date of record on it, and would take Aisling to the little grave in Maplewood, near the Arboretum, Sunday mornings in those first months of their bereavement. It was those Sunday visits to his dead son's grave that became the basis for the folio of poems, provisionally titled *Nativity*, which formed the core of a memoir she wrote the year following Nigel's death that was shortlisted for the Pulitzer and fast-tracked Aisling's tenure with the university. In the few years since, she had published another book of her own poems and a critical study of Nigel's work; she had read and lectured all over the country, from the Library of Congress to Huntington Library, and been featured in profiles on National Public Radio and PBS. Much as she tried to avoid the role of poetry's heartsore young widow, there was no doubt that her years with Nigel, her well-documented bereavements, and her relative youth and beauty made her something of an item on the literary circuit. She drew a crowd where others mostly drew a few. Her classes filled early at the university, with more young men than young women in them. Her poems, reviews, scholarly papers were all solicited by the better journals and magazines. Her fees for lectures and readings kept rising and rising. The invitations required the retention of a speaker's agent. She was even considering hiring a personal assistant – someone to help with the correspondence and calendar and travel details – but so far the right person hadn't materialized. Besides, she often thought, the daughter of a chief executive officer has sufficient management and discipline bred in the bone to handle a literary and academic career. Her celebrity, such as it was, had provided a secure income, the choice about how much work she would do and plenty of exciting opportunities, all within her range of expertise. She had exceeded her own expectations of herself, becoming not only a witness to artists but an artist herself. She was at forty both teacher and the subject taught, poet and critic and woman of substance.

She kept herself fit with the usual regimens. She gathered her long black and graying hair into a variety of buns and braids, updos and ponytails. She dressed in vintage ensembles mostly bought secondhand at the Salvation Army and she spent with abandon on designer shoes. She kept her distance from doctors, gardened in three seasons, took pills for insomnia and mild depression, smoked in private on occasion, and had a tattoo on her right buttock that matched the one on her late husband's left. They'd had them done in Spokane the April before moving to Ann Arbor with money they made from reading together. In the years since Nigel's death she had not had sex and seldom missed it. Sometimes she would take a long bath with scented candles and Chinese soaps and bring herself to orgasm. The knowledge that there were men who would still be eager and willing to have sex with her was, in some ways to Aisling, better than sex with any of them might eventually be, requiring as it would a degree of intimacy and theater she was not so certain she was even capable of. She had abandoned all prospects of parenthood, spoke to her aging father infrequently, and lived now at some little distance from her body and soul. If not entirely happy, she was content.

IT WAS the ad in the in-flight magazine for the Grand Hotel
that guided Aisling Black to Mackinac – the tiny island in
Lake Huron and the Straits of Mackinaw between Michigan's
upper and lower peninsulas. She'd been there with her father
as a child and remembered her enchantment with the place,
the enforced absence of automobiles, the busy docks and harbor, the horses and buggies and Victoriana, the easy opulence
of the hotel, the dress code for dinner, the afternoon teas and
string quartets. *Timeless* . . . read the banner over the photo of
the hotel. There was a website and phone number. She could
see herself doing nothing for a long time on the broad porch
of the great hotel, watching the inland sea sparkling in the
distance, restoring herself, renewing her stamina, readying
for the school term that would begin in September. After she
cleared customs in Detroit, she phoned the Grand, reserved
a lake-view room until the end of the month, drew cash from
an ATM in the terminal, got a seat on the five o'clock flight to
Pellston Airport, a cab twelve miles north to Mackinaw City,
where she was deposited along with her much-traveled bags at
the Arnold Line Docks, and after the brief ferryboat ride across
the Straits, she found herself on the island.

'Professor Black?' said a young man in footman's dress,
top-hatted and gloved, and when she nodded, he took her bag,
took her gently by the elbow, and led her to the shiny red-wine-
colored coach with *The Grand Hotel* stenciled in gilt italics on
the door. He looked like one of her undergrads, dressed for
the prom or student musical – *Great Expectations*, she thought,
Mr. Darby himself! He helped her into the coach, climbed up
to take the reins, and brought her by turns up through the

town to a wide thoroughfare which led uphill to the huge white clapboard edifice on the southwestern-facing bluff which was truly, now that she saw it aglow in the night, a grand hotel. The creak of the wooden coach, the strain of the draft horses up the hill past a stone church and wooden townhouses, the absence of anything automotive in the air – the racket of horns or emissions of motors – all of it conspired to slow her approach, after the furious day of taxis and airlines and ferries. It was, she knew, a kind of Disney, a theme park of sorts, a pretense of a place beyond the reach of real time. All the same, she could feel it almost metabolically – the pace of things slowing to the footfall of horses, of couples strolling the gaslit sidewalks or stretched out on the greensward listening to distant music – everything could wait, nothing was urgent, time could be taken, the moment held up for examination. She could feel herself getting sleepy. He took her immediately to her room, where a basket of fruits and cheeses and a bottle of wine had been left with a welcome note from the hotel's manager. He turned the light on in the bathroom, drew the curtains shut, placed her bags in the closet, and gave her the key to the room and honor bar. He said she could call the front desk in the morning about her registration. She could tell he could tell she was very tired.

'What time is it?' she asked him.

'Going ten. Where have you come to us from, Professor?'

'London, Detroit, well, Ann Arbor, by way of London today.'

'A long journey. You'll want a good night's sleep.'

'Yes, sleep's the thing.' She proffered a twenty-dollar bill.

'Oh no, Professor, I really couldn't. There's no tipping expected or permitted at the Grand. If there's anything at all, anything, just call . . . Enjoy your stay.'

He was out the door and she was left standing in the middle of a large corner room that looked out over the grounds of the hotel, the lakeshore and the Straits of Mackinaw, and in the distance, the lights of the Mackinaw Bridge, which connected the two peninsulas of her native state. She stripped and showered briefly, wrapped herself in the hotel robe, hugging herself in the plush terrycloth, savored a berry, left the wine untouched, then crawled under the down comforter, assembled the pillows according to custom, and considered the distance she'd come that day. Then Aisling Black fell into a sleep the details of which she would not remember. Whether she dreamed of her dead husband or baby, or new phantasms of love and desire, or random remnants from her travels: the pulsing in her temple, the usual insomnia, the cares of the day, all of it gave way to the blank oblivion of comfort and keen fatigue.

She woke briefly before dawn and did not know if she was fully awake or only between deeper slumbers. She rolled from one shoulder to the other, sat up in bed, and with gathering consciousness wondered if she oughtn't to make some notes toward an opening lecture for her senior seminar – a reading and writing course she taught to undergraduates in which she tried to get them to use the work of masters as predicates for their own creative efforts. *The Sincerest Form* was the title of a book one of her colleagues had written on the uses of imitation for young writers. She took it as the title of her course in the catalogue. Part of her lecture, indeed part of the paper she had recently delivered at the Yeats International Summer School, focused on the formulation, attributed to T. S. Eliot, that 'all poets borrow, great poets steal.' As evidence of this dictum she had produced W. B. Yeats's late nineteenth-century transcription of a late sixteenth-century sonnet by Pierre de Ronsard, 'pour Hélène.'

Quand vous serez bien vieille, au soir, à la chandelle,
Assise auprès du feu, dévidant et filant,
Direz, chantant mes vers, en vous émerveillant:
Ronsard me célébrait du temps que j'étais belle.

The poem, a cautionary tale to reticent lovers whose beauty will not outlive the lines of poems, is borrowed by Yeats to woo and warn his life's great and unattainable love, Maud Gonne.

When you are old and grey and full of sleep,
And nodding by the fire, take down this book,
And slowly read, and dream of the soft look
Your eyes had once, and of their shadows deep.

Aisling made her case that poetic license was, in fact, license to steal, in service of the art itself, from all the poems that have come before. All art, she would further argue, communes with all of the art that went before it. 'It's what we do', she'd say, quoting Auden, 'to break bread with the dead.' And she called on her students to become priests and priestesses of the holy forms of language and literature. She would regale them with the romance between Yeats and Maud Gonne, how he had pursued her and she had refused him, his many proposals, but kept up their 'intercourse' all of their lives. She would read them what he wrote in his journal on the day that he first saw her – the thirtieth of January, 1889: *I was twenty-three years old when the troubling of my life began.* And she would read them his breathless first description of her: *I had never thought to see in a living woman so great beauty. It belonged to famous pictures, to poetry, to some legendary past.*

Aisling knew that her students were similarly vexed, being

likewise in their early twenties, by the beauty and heartbreak they were finding in one another, and that their aptitudes for poetry and language might be, if she could attach them to their sharpening romantic and sexual appetites, forever fixed in their temperaments. Sex and death, she would always instruct them, are the only subjects worth thinking about. And then she would tell them she stole that from Yeats, who had written it in a letter to Olivia Shakespeare. Love and grief, she would further instruct them, share the one body. And she knew that they knew that this was true. She encouraged them to imitate the poems they most admired, to match them, as Yeats had with Ronsard, line for line, theme by theme, rhyme scheme by rhyme scheme, until they found themselves sounding more like themselves than like their dead or elder mentors. In fulfillment of which assignments she had received more of the ridiculous than the sublime – *Let us go then, you and I / Out for some brewskies and pizza pie* – but still she had them thinking about poetry as something they could not only read, but do. What matter if most of them ended up as marketing assistants and investment bankers, sales reps and attorneys – hers was to move them as best she could to become readers and writers, if not for a living, at least as accessories to their lives.

It was going toward daylight now and Aisling had papers from her briefcase spread on the bed. She scolded herself for abandoning her resolve to find deeper rest and so she turned off the nightlight, closed her eyes, and lay flat beneath the coverlet, touching herself, trying to recall what it was to be touched.

When she opened the curtains just before noon the light in her windows all but blinded her. She looked out eastward over the town and harbor to Round Island and Bois Blanc and the ferryboats plying the Straits from Mackinaw City and St.

Ignace. The small abandoned lighthouse at the harbor's mouth was one she had seen on postcards for years as an icon of Michigan's Great Lakes. To the southwest was the five-mile bridge between Michigan's peninsulas and beyond it the edge of Lake Michigan, its freshwater blue unlike any sea or ocean, sparkling in the mid-August light. She unlocked the bank of tall windows and opened them for the fresh blast of summer air and the rattle of horse-drawn traffic below. She looked around the large bedchamber with its nineteenth-century sofa and Queen Anne wingbacks and inlaid cherry writing table and straightback chair. There were cushioned window seats along the side windows, a queen-size four-poster bed, and tiled bathroom with Jacuzzi and glass shower stall. There were richly framed prints of seaside tableaux – Daubigny's *The Beach at Villerville*, Seurat's pointillist masterpiece of *La Grande Jatte*, and one she recognized as *September Morn*, of a nude girl standing ankle deep in the water, though she couldn't remember the artist's name. A bit too vivid and pastel for her tastes, she thought, all signature Carleton Varney. Nigel would never have slept in such a room; she winced at the little needle of guilt that such excess should be wasted on herself alone. Still, the views were spectacular, the feather bed had given her the best night's sleep she'd had in months, and the light, as she stood in it, was an ointment and balm to all that ailed her. She would make the best of her time here, whatever the cost was – it hardly mattered. She ordered breakfast and newspapers to the room, asked that the florist send up a centerpiece for the coffee table, set about putting away her things, and set up her laptop on the writing desk, determined to remain in the rented robe for most of the day. Much of the clothing she'd traveled to Europe with was all a little stale from the long journeys, overly wrinkled,

too dull for the midsummer ambience of her new surroundings. She examined the catalogue of hotel services and on-site
shops and found a serviceable outlet for women's fashions
in one of the first-floor boutiques. She'd pay a visit after her
brunch. She studied her feet and scheduled a pedicure with
the salon. She avoided the temptation to check her email or
call her father or make known to her colleagues in Ann Arbor
her whereabouts. She wanted to remain outside the loop and
range of the known and ordinary world and to bask in the
bright late-summer light, free of any obligation. She studied the
local directory for newsagents, bookstores, points of interest.
She resolved to rent a bike and see the island, named by the
Ojibwas for its turtle shape and regarded as sacred to the spirit
world. All in her own good time, she thought. But for now she
promised to do nothing of substance beyond growing accustomed to the space she inhabited. She breakfasted, dressed
casually in khaki slacks and a white blouse, wore sunglasses
and a ball cap, as if going incognito, and made her way out to
inspect her surroundings. By midafternoon she had registered
with the front desk, looked in the dining room and café and
terrace bar; she'd walked the length of the front porch – six
hundred and sixty feet: *Longest Porch in the World*, the signage
said – walked down to the pool and formal gardens, then back
to the hotel for the spa and some shopping. She had, in the
same time, acquired a new wardrobe, a new sense of wellness,
and a new appetite for whatever she might find on the menus.
She napped, and then surveyed the ensemble she'd bought in
the hotel's boutique. She'd splurged on a pair of strappy black
patent leather cork-soled wedges to go with her pedicure. She
found a simple black linen dress with a deep V neckline that
gathered softly just below her knees which she thought would

look perfect with the turquoise pashmina shawl she'd found in London. Near the checkout she found a pair of seed bead dangling earrings, also in turquoise, and a blue moiré water silk headband to match. For Aisling, each element of an ensemble was vested with meaning or metaphor or symbol, so that wearing it, she became an accessory, somehow, to a larger narrative the denouement of which remained unknown. Seeing the new garments laid out on the bed filled her with curiosity about her place in it all. She dressed in quiet, consulting the bureau mirror after every element of her outfit was added.

When she appeared in the lobby just after high tea, half an hour before dinner would be served, she looked rested and reborn. The hotel manager, a man in his thirties trying to look older than he was, standing sentinel in his blue suit and club tie and button-down shirt, hastened across the lobby to offer any assistance.

'Good evening, Mrs . . . ?'

'Black,' she told him, 'Aisling Black.'

He shook her hand and smiled earnestly.

'Is this your first visit to Grand Hotel?'

'My first in years' she said. 'I used to come here with my father for conventions. I remember him meeting the governor here. And I was here the year they were making the movie.'

'Yes, Jane Seymour and Christopher Reeve . . . how very sad . . . to think of him so damaged by falling from a horse . . . They made that movie in '79.'

'*Somewhere in Time*?' She had never seen it.

'That's it, *Somewhere in Time*, indeed.'

'I remember them filming in this lobby.'

'Well, you're welcome back after all these years. What is it you do now?'

'I write, I'm at the University of Michigan.'

'Yes, yes! *Professor* Black. I saw that you'd arrived last night. Mark Twain was here, you know . . . lectured on the front porch, July of 1895. Perhaps we could impose upon you to give a reading?'

'How very kind of you, but really, no, no, I'm here to be healed from all kinds of work.'

'Of course, Professor, I understand.'

'I'm Aisling, just Aisling, but thank you anyway.'

'I'm Michael Musser, my family has owned the place for years. Please let me know if there's anything, anything we can do to make your stay –'

'Thank you, Michael, I will of course.'

They had arrived at the entrance to the dining room.

'Would you like a cocktail before dinner, Profess – Aisling? It's early, what would you like?'

'Maybe a scotch?'

'And soda? Water?'

'No, only scotch. Then a table, the fresh air . . . I'm famished suddenly.'

'And will you be dining alone?'

She nodded and smiled.

He arranged with the maître d' of the dining room to seat her at a window table so that she could have a view of the porch, the grounds, and the lake. He brought her a tumbler of single malt, asked if he could get her anything else, promised to be at her beck and call, then left her to enjoy her dinner.

Aisling was used to dining alone. The time formerly spent conversing with Nigel between ordering and courses she now passed people-watching, assigning fictions to the assorted configurations at different tables. The elegant and amply mir-

rored dining room was a perfect venue for this, as people unaccustomed to dressing for dinner rose to the occasion of their
surroundings. Most of the families with school-age children
were back to their lives now, leaving the hotel and the island to
seniors and young couples and what seemed like a convention
of visiting engineers or architects. The whiskey warmed her.
A black man in a white dinner jacket brought her a menu. She
was happy to have something to hold and read as she watched
the tables fill. The mirrored columns that ran the length of
the long dining room allowed her to consider people at various
angles without appearing to stare. A woman with a goiter and
a fat husband, the pretty couple on their honeymoon, from
Pinconning, she imagined, where his family had made a little
fortune in cheese and hers farmed sugar beets. This was his first
suit and she'd been a virgin. Or maybe not, Aisling thought;
maybe he was home on leave from Afghanistan and she was
an escort from Traverse City, the long luxury weekend and
the hooker paid for by a kindly uncle who couldn't abide the
thought of the bright-faced boy going back to the war before
sleeping with a woman. Or maybe it was she who was home
and he the escort and a rich lesbian aunt who paid. The possibilities were inexhaustible. She loved to bask in the liberties
of fiction and thought she might like to write a novel. The four
blue-haired women, maybe sisters or widows from the same
Presbyterian church, here for a hospice conference or bridge
tournament. The handsome brothers and their fashionable
wives, men in their fifties, here to celebrate a mother's birthday
maybe? Anything was possible, or was not.

It was in the mirror, at an angle, that Aisling first saw the
young woman decanting water into glasses at a table slightly
behind her and slightly left. Whether it was the grace with

which she moved among them or the startling beauty of her face, unlike any Aisling had ever seen, or the poise and shapeliness of her figure, half hidden in a mannish dinner jacket, black trousers, white shirt and bow tie, it was hard to know; but Aisling heard herself catch her breath and her right hand moved to cover her mouth, which had opened to make the sound of vowels as she let the caught breath go. She was dressed to match the rest of the waitstaff except for the maître d' and headwaiters, who were dressed in tails. Hers was an apparently junior or apprenticed position as she never served food or wine and only cleared tables after they'd been vacated by diners. Her skin was mocha-colored and her eyes still blacker and her bearing was regal though she was not tall. And while she could have been a native Detroiter or Tanzanian, Aisling guessed she was Jamaican. Crews from that island nation had been coming to Mackinac for years, spending April until late October working at the Grand and then returning home for the winter season at the Wyndham Resort in Kingston. When she came to fill Aisling's water goblet the older woman blushed and feigned composure whilst the younger, whose name badge read *Bintalou*, smiled shyly and backed away. Though Aisling tried to appear engaged with the menu, she was in fact following her every move around the room, using mirrors for the wider scrutiny they provided. Nothing on the menu, from the 'Braised Pork and Vegetable Spring Roll in Ginger-Mushroom Soy Sauce' appetizer to the 'Almond-Macadamia Crusted Trout' entrée could take her attention from the beauty. When the waiter asked Aisling what she had decided on, she ordered another scotch and told him to choose something for her; everything on the menu looked sumptuous and she'd trust his instincts. Bintalou was sixteen or seventeen, Aisling

guessed, and near enough Aisling's own size – just over five feet
and a hundred pounds. Their eyes were near enough the same
color, though the girl's were deeper, darker, entirely benign. Her
black hair was braided in tight cornrows and her bosom and
her bottom were rounder, higher, more ample and sinewy than
Aisling's, and her body was bolder, more powerful. She had tiny
wrists, long, delicate fingers, thin arms, perfect ankles. Her
blackness was richer, more articulate, than Aisling's whiteness.
The newness of it, its purity and youth, its incarnate beauty
were utterly compelling. Aisling could feel the heat of a blush
rising just watching the girl move about the room among the
clatter of dinnerware and conversations, the industry of the
waitstaff, the piano music in the corner, the chandeliers and
candlelight – everything was silent and incidental to the aura
and cocoon of luminary beauty her vision moved in.

The girl's connection to the maître d' was a curiosity. He
paid her a great deal of attention, seeming to instruct her at
every opportunity. The obvious deference paid by the other
servers was, Aisling reckoned, connected to this.

Aisling nursed the second tumbler of scotch slowly, and
picked indifferently at the choices the waiter had made, a
spinach salad with pecans and goat cheese and dried cherries
and an entrée of wild mushroom ravioli. She kept hoping the
girl would come to refill her water glass or clear the plates from
her table, but as the dining room filled, it became clear the
Jamaicans worked in teams, working separate sections of the
dining room, and that Bintalou was assigned to one nearer
the main entrance. Aisling ordered a dessert, the better to
extend her silent audience. And after dessert, she chose a
brandy, Calvados Coquerel, to tarry all the longer.

She had watched the light go out of the day, replaced by a

full moon that lit the surface of the Straits below. And because
the evening was fine and warm, she decided to walk the long
porch after dinner while other guests lazed in the wicker rock-
ers that lined the porch on one side, with the planters of red
geraniums on the other. Even from the outside, with the lights of
the bridge and the village below and the moonlight on the water
all around, Aisling was focused on the interior as she walked,
looking through windows for the girl moving among the last of
the evening's dinner guests.

Aisling's sleep that night was vexed by dreams of her dead
husband and son. She had not taken a pill to sleep because
she'd been drinking. The night was fitful and she woke full
of longing – though she could not say exactly for what. She
wondered if she'd be able to make two weeks. She took a long
shower and dressed for a day of walking. Downstairs she made
her way into the dining room, not so much for breakfast as to
read the papers and to see if the girl was working the breakfast
shift. She recognized the waitstaff from the night before but
there was no sign of Bintalou. Better to take her beauty sleep,
Aisling thought, and ordered orange juice and toast and coffee.

The papers were full of the coming elections, worries over
the local and national economy, the crisis in home mortgages
and foreclosures, the falling values in the automotive stocks. A
large portion of her own trust fund was held in General Motors
stock since they were the largest purchaser of her father's safety
glass. In the first nine months of the year the stock had lost
half its value. The prospect loomed that the company would
be bankrupt before the year was out and that her little fortune
would be seriously diminished. The stock of her father's company, the other large portion of her trust fund, had also lost
considerable value.

Aisling had always adopted a style between the struggling artist and the sensibly situated academic, but she was comforted by the knowledge that wealth, inherited from her father, but wealth all the same, spared her the common worries over livelihood and future and freed her from daily interest in the marketplace. She was raised in privilege and was accustomed to ignoring the politics and economics of the larger world in deference to her intellectual and artistic pursuits. She wondered if the 'one-state recession' that the papers claimed Michigan was in, because of the 'failing domestic automotive industry', would actually have an effect on her. She had seen it in Europe – the comparative devaluation of the dollar, the higher costs of everything, the fears among retailers and hoteliers. The ongoing wars, the distrust of American leadership, the global markets in disarray, the price of oil – there had even been a surcharge on the ferryboat over to the island, blamed on the cost per gallon of gasoline. And now that she looked about the room, she could see that here in high season, the middle of August, in the finest hotel in Michigan, many of the tables were empty at breakfast, much as the seats on the ferry over had been. Even the hotel's 'Modern Baroque' décor, reconsidered in the morning light, with its striped wallpapers and floral print chintz, by Dorothy Draper's celebrated protégé, seemed now a little dated and overwrought – the old century's effort to update the century before. The table settings of Syracuse china, 'since 1871–USA', now that she looked closely, were faded and dull, and the Irish linen tablecloths frayed and somewhat overlaundered. As she looked around the room half filled with elderly visitors wearing the name badges of conventioneers and senior tours, eating their omelets and oatmeal and fruits, the grandeur of the Grand Hotel seemed to Aisling perhaps a little past its prime. Perhaps the economy really was in serious peril, Aisling thought, and marveled that she should live to be forty before such a thought ever occurred to her. The first needle of a headache stabbed her right temple. She sipped her water, closed her eyes, inhaled deeply.

The merchants she gossiped with in town that morning all ranged between commiseration and denial. Oh sure, the season's traffic was a little off, nothing to panic over, the crowds would return once the price of gasoline went down. The local fudge shops still made big slabs of the local specialty on marble altars in the shopwindows. The liveries renting riding horses and carriages or offering guided tours of the island still kept the downtown sounding like an old western with hoofbeats on the pavement. The auto industry had been failing for years – laboring under its pension and health care costs, executive salaries, poor decisions about consumer preferences. Mackinac relied on its six hundred horses – hackneys and drafts and even-tempered riding stock – for taxi and tours and haulage. The rich smell of fried food and horse manure was a welcome change from the diesel smell of London and Belfast, and the soft breeze off the big water made it all bearable under the August sun. Aisling wore a smart panama and sunglasses, walking shorts and a blue denim shirt, and browsed among the souvenir shops with nothing in mind. She listened to a trio – guitar and fiddle and hammered dulcimer – playing bluegrass music in front of one of the Main Street hotels. She walked the docks of the marina in the harbor where sailing boats tethered to their buoys and power yachts snug in their berths shone in the sparkling water. She bought sunscreen and applied it and walked up the town among the day-trippers.

At the end of Main Street was a large village green overseen by a life-size bronze of Jacques Marquette, in soutane and cape, atop a tall granite base. He was among the first Europeans to see the Straits and wintered on the island in 1670, disabusing the native Huron and Ojibway of their heathenry. Aisling sat on a bench among the families and sunbathers sprawled on the green and read from a pocket history she bought at the bookstore:

> *Father Jacques Marquette, the great Jesuit missionary and explorer, died and was buried by two French companions somewhere along the Lake Michigan shore on May 18, 1675. He had been returning to his mission at St. Ignace, which he had left in 1673 to go exploring in the Mississippi country. The exact location of his death has long been a subject of controversy. A spot close to the southeast slope of a hill, near the ancient outlet of the Pere Marquette River, corresponds with the death site as located by early French accounts and maps and a constant tradition of the past. Marquette's remains were reburied at St. Ignace in 1677, when Hurons disinterred his remains and bore his bones back in a cedar box.*

She read about the ancient fishing tribes, remnants of which, dating to the tenth century, had been found, who thought of the island as the home of 'Gitche Manitou' – the Great Spirit. And about the fur trade and John Jacob Astor's export of beaver pelts from the island. She read about how it became the second national park in 1875, after Yellowstone, and later was given to Michigan as its first state park.

Above the green on a bluff overlooking the harbor was Fort Mackinac, a limestone encampment built by the British in 1780 to control the Straits during the Revolutionary War. I'll tour

that another day, she told herself, avoiding her natural temptation to scholarship instead of rest and lazing. She repeated
her resolve to do nothing of substance and blamed the sudden
return of her headache on reading through sunglasses or too
much sun. She decided to walk back to the Grand, maybe nap
for an hour, and then maybe a swim.

It was coming out of a three-story green clapboard house
– one of the dormitories for Grand Hotel staff – on Cadotte
Avenue that Aisling saw Bintalou, dressed in traditional housekeeping attire and making her way with a young man, arm
in arm towards the Grand. As lovely as she'd been the night
before, in the late-morning light she was more beautiful still.
Her blackness shone. Her stride was athletic and elegant and
her pace lengthened the distance between her and Aisling as
they walked uphill. Try as she might, Aisling could not catch
up to the girl and her companion. She became aware of her
windedness and fatigue, which combined with her now throb-
bing headache to become a little panic, plodding up the east
side of the boulevard while the object of her deepest interest
strode up the west. The young man she walked with wore the
top hat and red frock coat of the Grand's carriage drivers. In
every other way unprepossessing, he was not tall, nor handsome, nor did he seem especially gifted, except that he was
walking next to her. Aisling couldn't say for certain if they were
simply companions or actually lovers. They seemed impossibly
young for the mysteries of it all. Still, Aisling had read enough
undergraduate papers to know that few of her students came to
university as virgins. Their compositions often included cheer-
ful narratives of 'hook-ups' and 'fuck buddies', 'friends with
benefits' and variations on the theme – sex-for-the-sake-of-sex
encounters, unencumbered by deeper meanings, detached

from feelings beyond a general fondness. This was at odds with Aisling's upbringing and experience, which assigned to every touch or caress, kiss or entanglement a meaning and purpose and direction. That she could no longer make out the manifest cues of one body's relations with another disturbed her greatly. Perhaps it was due to her own sexual circumstance, whereby, with the exception of the years with Nigel, she labored between spasms of ineptitude and decrepitude – conditions that rhymed too perfectly to ever include in one of her poems.

By the time she reached the lobby of the Grand, Bintalou had already assumed her station in the Salle à Manger, tending to the endless luncheon buffet, and the young man, true to his uniform, was sitting atop one of the hotel coaches under the main entrance portico, much like the one that had transported her hither from the docks the night of her arrival. But for the piercing pain behind her eyes, she would have gone in for a long lunch and the chance to watch the beauty move among the fruits and soups, coldcuts and pastries. Instead she went up to her room, drew the drapes, and took a nap.

In what remained of her two weeks at the Grand, Aisling's infatuation with the Jamaican girl only grew more fervid and consuming. She woke every morning with a plan to pursue chance encounters. She hid her quizzing of Michael Musser, ever the helpful host, about his hotel and waitstaff, in sufficiently innocuous banter so as to avoid concerns. She came early to the dinner service at night and almost always stayed until the end, lingering over desserts and coffees, then taking up her watch on the east end of the long porch, hoping to see Bintalou exit by the service door below, whereupon she would hasten to follow her to what she knew was her room in the front right corner of the third floor of the green house at the bottom of Cadotte Avenue. By turns she had come to know the girl's routines and haunts, her variable schedule and her days off. She'd found out that Bintalou was, indeed, the daughter of the dining room's major-domo. The distinguished-looking man in tails and vest – Henry Goodison – was in charge of seating and oversaw the gloved waiters and the lesser servers. He had been working summers in the Salle à Manger for forty years and was, to the Mussers, central to the smooth dispensation of service. Henry Goodison had been the ideal head man and factotum. Honest, loyal, proud in his bearing, and a natural leader. Not only had he a memory for the names of returning guests, but he would ask about their children and children's children, all the while displaying the crisp efficiency and stewardship of his position. He'd become the natural liaison between the Mussers and the Jamaicans, settling disputes over wages and scheduling and monitoring the conduct of his countrymen in their off hours to prevent any scandal or disruptions. His only lapse in perfect conduct was a generation ago, when he had impregnated one of the housekeeping staff, the daughter of his neighbor in Kingston. Bintalou had been raised by her mother, alone, inasmuch as Mr. Goodison already had a wife and family. He had been supportive financially, but otherwise kept his distance. And only when Bintalou's mother died had she come to stay with the Goodisons. Her father's long history of coming and going between the Caribbean and Mackinac Island had made it possible for Bintalou to get a visa for the summer – a far more difficult thing, according to Michael Musser, since the attacks of September 11. Indeed, much of the summer help on Mackinac now was Polish or Mexican or Ukrainian. Only the dining room of the Grand remained the province of the West Indians. The Mussers had promised Henry Goodison a room and board for his daughter and part-time work and training –

her age, fifteen, making a full-time position quite impossible. Besides, it gave her time to be with other young people from around the world and from Michigan, and provided her father the chance to reconnect with her and gave her plenty of time off to enjoy the new environs.

Aisling's fascination with the girl was outside the range of all former experience and, she believed, at odds with her orientation and discipline. The two or three same-sex romances she had had as an undergraduate were, for the most part, exploratory, as much to satisfy curiosities for her partners as for herself. She was, if not recently, nonetheless a heterosexual. Her dreams conformed, her memories. She missed the sound of Nigel's strong piss in the toilet in the morning, the scratch of his razor over his face, the smell of him – whiskey and tobacco. She missed his mannish foibles and self-certainties. She missed his love. His desire.

Her growing fantasies in which Bintalou figured so prominently owed, she reasoned, to a confluence of longings – for a child, for a lover, for a life of passion and meaning beyond the meager rehearsals of her own. The stunning young Jamaican, Aisling further reckoned, was the embodiment of all that she'd pursued as an artist and a scholar – a beauty beyond the idea of beauty, rather the living, breathing incarnation of beauty itself. This prospect frightened and excited her.

When she finally and with some regret asked Mr. Musser to prepare her final bill, on the evening before her scheduled departure, he said he'd be sad to see her go and hoped that she'd be a regular visitor in summers to come. He said he would organize a car to meet her at the dock in Mackinaw City and drive her to the airport in Pellston in plenty of time to make her flight to Detroit.

Aisling Black left the Grand in the early morning, a fog with the first chill hint of autumn in it hovering over the harbor. She got an early ferry, watched as the boat turned out of the harbor and the great white edifice of the Grand came into view. 'Bintalou', she whispered to herself, then turned her sights on the distant mainland.

The man holding the sign on the docks with her name on it threw her bags in the back of his rusting brown minivan, and said that there'd been a slight change of plans. He was sorry to report that her flight from Pellston was canceled.

'Mustn't have been enough seats bought up. They always blame it on the weather or some 'mechanicals.' But it's dollars and cents, simple as that, ma'am. No sense spending all that jet fuel on less than a full flight.'

'But I have a ticket, I have to get home. I have classes in Ann Arbor tomorrow.'

'Not to worry, ma'am, I've thought of that. I can have you back south in no time. Hell, Ann Arbor's four hours. Door to door, faster than the jet, what with all the security and searches and waiting around and crap. And I'll charge you less.' He was holding the door of the minivan, and beckoning with the other arm for her to sit in for the drive south.

'No . . . no, that's not what I planned on. You don't understand. I've a splitting headache; I can't take four hours on the road. I have a ticket and reservation. I'm sorry, just take me to the airport.'

'No sense in going to the airport, ma'am, the flight has been canceled, you can check for yourself.' He held out his cell phone. 'I have 'em on speed dial. I'm trying to be helpful here. I'll charge you less than the airlines, ma'am. A hundred and fifty, no need to tip. Hell, the gas will cost me nearly that.'

Now Aisling's head was pounding and she was confused. She didn't want to get in his car. The other passengers were making their way to the car park. They had their own vehicles and places to go. She backed up and sat down on the bench by the boat. She was feeling pushed to a decision she didn't want to make. How could she get in a car with a perfect stranger? Why would the airlines cancel a flight? The day was clearing. Conditions were fine. Why should she have to change her plans?

'I'm sorry, I can't go now. It's quite impossible. Kindly leave me my bags.' She took a twenty-dollar bill from her purse. 'For your trouble, please . . . I really can't go. I won't. Impossible.'

'Whatever you say, ma'am. Customer's always right.' And he muttered something under his breath. He refused the gratuity and left her bags beside her and got in his minivan and drove away.

After a few moments to gather herself, Aisling moved to the shade of the Arnold Line ticket office. She sat in the pavilion wondering what it was she should feel. Outrage? Relief? A secret thrill? When questioned by the ticket agent about her plans, she bought a one-way ticket for the ten o'clock boat to the island and retraced her morning's journey back to the hotel.

When she presented herself in Michael Musser's office, he congratulated her on the decision to stay. He was sorry for the trouble in traveling but pleased that it had returned her to the Grand. The room she had vacated was being tidied for another incoming guest but he would find her a room as fine or nicer for the same rate as her old room. She was welcome at the Grand for as long as she'd like. He took her up on the elevator to inspect the suite.

'A stroke of luck', he said when she approved the new

quarters. 'We had a cancellation this very morning. It's the economy. Like a plague. No confidence. Everyone is cutting back. Of course, they always claim a death in the family, or a sickness. I understand.' Then, catching himself as the purveyor of doom, he made hasty apologies and backed out of the room.

Aisling settled herself in the tall wingback chair by the bank of windows that looked out to the Straits, amazed at the morning's happenstance, and a little peeved at herself for her vacillations, irked at her ignorance of her own desires. She would have to let the department know about her delay in returning. She composed the email in her head, not wanting to talk to the department in person. She would amplify the matter of a canceled flight and hope that no one thought it strange that she had stranded herself within two hundred and fifty miles of the university. How, after all, could she explain herself to them. She could hardly make sense of it all. She could have rented a car herself, driven down the interstate at a leisurely pace and been home before evening. Both her graduate workshop and undergraduate seminar met once a week for a three-hour session. So after missing the first week's duties tomorrow, she'd have a full week to get herself reconfigured and make her way home. She sat trying to clear her mind of contingencies and nodded off in the wingback into a restless sleep.

NOW THE poet gave herself over to the chance unwinding of the days before her and to the pursuit of beauty outside of the forms her training and temperament had always used. Rather than put the hours to work over sonnets or sestinas or the further cataloguing of her husband's work, rather than plan further lectures, assignments, classroom exercises or review

her students' writing samples, rather than send new work out
to the better journals or plan a conference for the coming year,
she sat for hours gazing at the water and the way the daylight
worked upon it. She succumbed to her preoccupation with
the young Jamaican, working her schedule around the girl's
schedule. When she was working the afternoon teas, Aisling
partook of the afternoon teas. When she was working the dining room, Aisling lingered there. When she was out for the day
with the young coachman, Aisling just followed on foot as the
young couple shopped among the stalls in town, or toured the
massive summer 'cottages' – Queen Annes and Greek Revivals
and Carpenter Gothics – on bluffs overlooking both ends of
town. These were summer homes with names like 'Far View'
and 'Tootle Cottage', 'Ingleneuk' and 'Windermere', built by
the moguls of another age, Midwest capitalists who made their
fortunes in textiles or railroads, lumber or banking; doctors
and soldiers and clergymen. The cupolas and turrets, widow's
walks and towers rose over the broad porches to look out on
Lake Huron and the Straits and west of the great bridge in
the distance, all down the long blue edge of summer in Michigan. Aisling, of course, tried to keep her distance, but it wasn't
long before she could tell that Bintalou and her paramour –
though of that she was not yet certain – had become aware of
her pursuit. There was no good way to explain how it was she
was always happening to be in their vicinity. What would she
eventually tell whoever it was who might eventually ask? That
she was transfixed by the vision of the girl; that the girl seemed
in every one of her aspects, utterly sublime, and that since gazing upon her beauty, all other ruminations on the theme of
beauty seemed poor imitations and wastes of time. She had
made studies in her notebook, hoping to draw out some verse

on this theme, but it was useless. On the subject of beauty
Aisling could wax eloquent, but in the presence of it she was
smitten to silence. All she could do was follow on, solitary in
her pursuit, hoping to get some succor for the hunger it whet-
ted in her for more of the same. She had grown more sleep-
less, more mindless of her resolve to rest, more mindful of the
madness the girl had ignited in her. But she was helpless to do
anything about it. She asked the hotel physician for a palliative
for her constant headache, which now only sharpened when the
girl was nowhere to be found. Aisling had confined her time
downstairs in the hotel to the times Bintalou was working. On
the girl's days off, Aisling searched out her whereabouts, checking the hotel environs first, often asking one of the coachman's
fellow drivers where might Blake Shields be that day – for she
had researched his name and other particulars – knowing that
they would likely be together.

The daily papers were full of concerns over the mortgage
crisis and home foreclosures. While waiting for a sighting of
Bintalou late one morning, Aisling Black sat out on the hotel
porch reading about the steep decline in home values over the
recent months – some by as much as 25 per cent – and the
'negative equity' many homeowners now had in their properties.
There were gathering worries over banking and insurance, the
stock market losses near 40 per cent, and the rising rate of
unemployment over 7 per cent across the country, nearing 10 per
cent in Michigan. Aisling could only wonder what it all meant,
having never considered the threat of ruin. She couldn't help
noticing the declining occupancy at the Grand. A rear section of
the dining room was now closed off. The hotel's usual numbers
of guests and staff seemed in decline. There were fewer golfers
on the golf course, swimmers in the pool, revelers in the bars,

old-timers at tea. The traffic in bikes and horse buggies was noticeably thinner. The fudge shops were closing earlier, the ferryboat schedules condensing, the souvenir shops discounting their trinkets, first by 10 per cent, then by 25. The days were growing shorter irretrievably.

One night after the dining room had closed Aisling followed Bintalou and Henry Goodison and Blake Shields to the ferry docks, where they took the boat over to St. Ignace, the nearest port on the Upper Peninsula. Aisling could not help but follow, so much had it become her custom now, seating herself several rows behind the trio on the lower deck of the ferry and following them from the dockside to the casino that was their destination. It was owned by the Chippewa Indians and offered banks of slot machines, keno, roulette and poker, blackjack and craps. She watched as they settled into their games. She took a seat at the blackjack table next to the one where the headwaiter was playing and Bintalou was sipping a soda behind him. Blake Shields was trying his luck with nickel slots. Aisling was perfectly positioned to watch the girl overlooking her father's cards, her face changing with his changing fortunes. Henry Goodison was well known and evidently well regarded in St. Ignace. Suited officials from the casino's management came over to greet him on their rounds. Cocktail waitresses brought him drinks. Several of his fellow gamers stopped to pay respects. He introduced them all to his daughter, who seemed more than delighted to be out with her dad, hugging him around his shoulders, kissing his large ears, and cheering when he won, offering consolations when he lost. Aisling envied their easy endearments, having long since grown distant from her own father. She found it hard to concentrate on the cards she was being dealt and kept losing more money than she ever intended, but was enthralled, nonetheless, with the proximity of the beautiful child and the games of chance. Aisling was amazed at the crowd of gamblers packed into the igloo-shaped casino. They were elderly, many were disabled, some of them looked near the edge of ruin. She imagined herself among them, in a venue out of Dante as people wagered not from their plenty but from their want. And in among the blinking lights and flashing machinery, Bintalou and her distinguished father hugged and giggled and smiled as he won.

It was after the last ferryboat back to the island by the time Henry Goodison was ready to call it a night. Aisling followed the trio to the docks, where they invited her to share a ride back on a private boat and to split the cost of the passage with them. It was as near as Aisling had ever been to the girl, who smiled shyly but kept up her talk with her father in their own patois, which was, like all local brogues and dialects, indecipherable to their fellow travelers.

'Greek to me, too', said Blake Shields, seeing Aisling straining to make some sense of the Jamaicans' talk. 'I get bits and pieces of it now and then.' He was trying to be courteous, leaning in closely to be heard in the open boat taking them back to the island. 'Are you enjoying your stay on the island?'

Aisling praised the peace and tranquillity, confessed that she'd stayed past her time, had missed another week of classes downstate but couldn't seem to work up the will to leave. He told her he'd be leaving in a week, that the community college he went to in Petoskey always started later because all the students worked the season in northern Michigan.

'What about your girlfriend?' Aisling asked, as if she were only making conversation.

'Binta?' he said, as if it wasn't certain, the nature of their relationship. 'She's missed a week already too. She attends an all-girls college – really it's a high school – in Jamaica. But her father's letting her stay until I leave next week. My folks will get her to the airport.'

The young man kept talking about how he had a bad case of island fever, couldn't wait to get back to the mainland, was disappointed with the tips this summer – 'Everyone's down 20, 30 per cent' – but Aisling was elsewhere in her private thoughts. She was looking out into the dark water as the hum of inboard motor dulled their voices. She was thinking of what she would do without her, trying to imagine them both back to their separate lives. She closed her eyes and could see young schoolgirls in the Lesser Antilles where Nigel had taken her over Christmas and New Year's not long after the pregnancy. He'd rented a villa overlooking Cruz Bay on the smallest of the U.S. Virgin Islands. She could see Bintalou now, as she remembered them, black schoolgirls in their baggy uniforms – yellow cotton blouses over pleated blue skirts, loose neckties, and white anklets – moving like pretty schools of fish in unison through the village on their way to and from school, mornings, afternoons, how he had been so perfectly solicitous of her, so tender, bringing her orchids and poems and bottled water, trying to hasten her heart's slow healing.

IN THE fourth week of her stay on Mackinac, Professor Aisling Black made certain observations about the world around her. The panic in the press, local and national, was growing more fraught with every day. There were rumors of banks on the brink of collapsing, an insurance carrier and a well-known investment house had bellied up, the candidates for the coming elections were full of dire predictions and promises. 'Toxic assets' and 'derivatives' had entered the talk among towns-people and merchants. The manicurist in the hotel salon told Aisling that last week a family of guests had been asked to leave when the fees for their stay far exceeded the limit on the credit card they'd provided at check-in. A yacht in the harbor had been repossessed: everywhere were signs of what the woman called 'a contagion' among the moneyed set. And while Aisling's own interests had never included money or concerns over solvency, her instincts as a scholar triggered an appetite for researchable data. She spent a day on the Internet examining the financial press and their websites, emailing her own accountant, checking her online bank accounts. She would have called her father but they'd grown distant over the years since her mother's death and she could not imagine a conversation that would allow either one of them to re-engage.

What was worse was the knowledge of Bintalou's coming departure. Aisling tried to imagine her life after the girl was gone. She had come to see herself almost entirely as an acolyte to the incarnate beauty.

By now she had figured out the predictable elements of Bintalou's routines. She knew, for example, that Sunday mornings would find her at worship in the Little Stone Congregational Church on the edge of the golf course between her dormitory lodge and the hotel. And though Aisling had given up any practice of religion, she attended the services, sang the old hymns along with the faithful, was generous when the basket was passed, and watched closely as the light through the stained glass illumined the angelic visage of her beloved. The pastor of the church was a man with a trained preaching voice, a toupee, and a precision about his clerical dress which, like the rest of the island, labored to seem from ages past. He preached about the gifts of the body and the spirit – good health and contentedness, fitness and fidelity – 'things beyond the purchase of any treasure!' Then he led the congregation in song, their voices rising to 'Softly and Tenderly Jesus Is Calling', which Aisling sang with real conviction and during which Bintalou, singing along with the rest of the church, turned and looked Aisling deep in her eyes, which had gone blurry with tears at the penultimate verse of the hymn:

> Time is now fleeting, the moments are passing,
> Passing from you and from me;
> Shadows are gathering, deathbeds are coming,
> Coming for you and for me.

That is when she knew that the long weeks of her pursuit of beauty might soon be coming to an end.

Thereafter, like any lover preparing to please her lover, Aisling took more time with her selection of costume, accessories, jewelry, and fragrance. She spent abundantly in the hotel shops and spa, in the latter of which she gave herself over to a full day of ministrations, from the Age Defying Purification Facial to the Herbal Stimulating Body Wrap and Hot Stone Massage. Considering herself in the full-length mirror, wrapped in a terrycloth and satin towel, the sight of her graying hair made her grimace.

When she returned to her room, coiffure and cosmetics perfectly done, she seemed a much-restored version of herself, from years before, in the weeks and months of her courtship with Nigel, readied and willing and eager to love. A version of the future that continued to take shape in Aisling's imagination was the one that involved an approach to Henry Goodison and the offer to take his daughter on as her personal assistant. The girl could come to live with her in Ann Arbor. The house in Burns Park was surely sufficient. Aisling would enroll the girl in Greenhills School, one of the best preparatory academies in the country, and eventually, of course, at the university. She would further agree to winter holidays in Jamaica and summers on Mackinac, but Bintalou would get the best of educations, eventual citizenship, a generous stipendium, and better prospects for the future. She could assist Aisling with the household duties, cooking and correspondence, shopping and social obligations. She would travel with Aisling on the widening circuit of literary duties, seeing the country and the world. It would be a remarkable tuition for a young woman and increase her own chances measurably; surely Henry would see the wisdom in all of this. Surely he'd want what was best for his daughter. They could share mealtimes, intellectual pursuits, even clothing – Aisling was sure all her things would fit – daily hopes and little heartbreaks. She could become the sister, daughter, mother, and partner, now that she thought of it, she never had. It was hereabouts that the revelation of this plan would begin to obscure itself in Aisling's contemplations.

It was mid-September – long past the time she should have returned to school – when the professor rented one of the hotel's bicycles and followed at a distance while Bintalou and her young coachman rode ponies out to the north side of the island. All the August crowds were gone. The senior-citizen tours remained in town, taking in the blacksmith's shop and Beaumont Museum, browsing for bargains in the stores, rummaging among the kitsch and knock-offs, the replicas of former treasures, the knick-knacks and copied curios.

By the time they turned northwestward around Mission Point, out past the Arch Rock and Voyageur's Bay, there was no one on the road but the pair on horseback and Aisling on her bike in pursuit. The late morning was warm and windless and bright blue, the lake water glistening and smooth. Aisling felt like a girl again on the Schwinn coaster pedaling along Lake Shore Road, further and further from the town. It was four miles to Point aux Pins – the tail of the turtle the island was shaped like – and as Aisling turned south she found the ponies tied to a picnic table off the road. This end of the island was heavily forested with white cedars and silver birches and the land pushed out overlooking the lake. Aisling settled her bike in the woods and walked through the trees toward the water past the remnants of an abandoned log cottage, coming to a high promontory out of which trees grew at angles and the land beneath gave way to a high bank going down to the lake. She could hear their voices rising up from below. There was no sign of the footpath they must have taken and Aisling was about to double back to the old cottage to see if she could find a way when she considered the base of a cedar tree growing out at an angle of forty-five degrees and another one next to it, their dense branches interlacing forming something of a natural observatory. Crawling out astraddle the trunk of the one tree, first balancing off the other tree, then bending forward to embrace the first, she found herself hidden in the leaning trees fifty feet above a patch of sandy beach the couple below her had found on an otherwise rocky shoreline. The outgrowth of arbor vitae, its flat filigree spray of leaves, provided perfect cover. She could see them and could not be seen.

Bintalou had brought a little lunch of fruit and cheeses from the Grand's buffet and from the same backpack produced some bottled water and a pair of towels. After eating they both stood, as if on signal, removed their shorts and T-shirts, their white undergarments, folded them carefully in the towels, and together, quite naked, ran into the lake wearing only their shoes because the bottom was rocky. Their shouts rose upward from the shock of water.

'It's cold!' cried Bintalou.

'Dive in', he called back, 'you'll get used to it!'

Aisling's limbs tightened her embrace of the tree and edged a little forward for a better view, the bark of the white cedar scratching her knees.

They were so gorgeous in the water, her perfect blackness, his perfect white, his blondness, her dark brunette, their buttocks and genitalia, those lovely, unspeakably perfect breasts. She could hardly breathe now that she saw the girl standing ankle deep in the shallows, bent ever so slightly forward, her left hand on her right elbow, hugging herself, her right hand in between her knees trying to warm itself, or cover herself – she could not say – looking off in the distance at the Les Cheneaux. Aisling's eyes were tearing up, her vision blurring; she was so grateful now for everything. Eventually the girl dove headlong into the deeper water and swam out to meet her companion, the two of them playing like children at the lake, trying to dunk one another, splashing each other, laughing, their bodies shining in the light and water.

Aisling considered climbing back to the land, finding her way down to the beach to join them, organizing excuses for how she had just 'happened upon this place', all very innocent and serendipitous. She would remove her own clothes as she approached them so as not to make them uncomfortable, so as not to make them cover themselves. She wanted to be naked with them, to tell them everything, to hear their histories and to tell them hers, how the heart bears its unspeakable cargo to lay it down at the feet of beauty.

But she could not move, she could not speak, her eyes were closing with her own arousal. She hugged the tree more passionately, pressing herself against its thickened bark. She felt her pulse rising in every vessel, behind her eyes, in her temples, in her limbs.

Whether she saw them or dreamed them or prayed for them to step from the water and lie on the beach beside one another in the midday sun, their heads on the pillows they had made of their clothes, first touching one another with such tenderness, then taking one another unto themselves; whether it happened as she saw it or did not see it, she could not know. Whether it was the lapping of lake water or the caught breath between them, their own entanglements or hers alone, she could not be certain. It hardly mattered. She lay in the soft embrace of the cedars, her arms and legs gone limp, her cheek turned softly against the tree. Whether ecstasy or aneurysm, apocalypse or broken heart, seizure, stroke, or *coup de chance*; whether every beauty echoes another – one's innocence, all art – whether to live for it or die for it, no longer mattered. The vision before her seemed to beckon, though her own vision was doubled, blurred by the leafy shade and light, her tears, the body or bodies, or souls – she could not know. She could feel her embrace of the cedar loosening. Her body and her being letting go.

Apparition

I

IT WAS *Good Riddance* that put Adrian Littlefield on the lecture circuit. Before *Riddance* he'd self-published two pastel-covered self-help books with fashionably gerundive titles – *Learning to Love in the Present Tense* and *Making the Best of Worst-Case Scenarios*. They were widely ignored and only sold to his family and folks at the church where he was the assistant pastor in those early years of marriage and parenthood. He'd done a workbook on dividing family duties between spouses and written a couple of articles for the ministerial press but otherwise was going nowhere and barely making ends meet until, after Clare left him, he wrote *Good Riddance – Divorcing for Keeps* and it changed his life.

It held that some divorces, like some marriages, are made in heaven. And we ought to be thankful for them. The key to living in concert with God's Will or the Natural Order or what the Fates had in mind for you was to learn to accept the direction your love life was taking you, even when it meant the end of love. Divorce was neither the result of too much of one thing nor too little of another, too many heartbreaks or too few. It was, like tsunamis and famines, hurricanes and genocides, God's way of culling humanity's herd of lovers, for reasons that were unknowable to mortals, but part, nonetheless, of a larger plan. Shit happens – Adrian Littlefield told his readers unambiguously – we must go with the flow. That's life, get over it, get on with it.

It took him six months to write it, a month to get an agent, and another month to get a contract and a fat advance from a publisher in New York. It was an immediate hit. The first printing sold out in a week. The paperback rights went for half a million. There was talk of a documentary for one of the cable networks.

The invitations followed. He worked up a little forty-minute shtick for the keynotes and workshops. He could bend his presentation, peppered with tastefully suggestive humor, around the occupational curiosities of any professional association. He had an infomercial in postproduction – one of those hour-long specials where he wore baggy clothes and did a little chalk talk with a really attractive and earnest-looking studio audience. He traveled three months out of every four from his home office in Findlay, Ohio, where he housed, behind his sprawling redbrick Queen Anne mansion on the corner of South Main and Second Streets, in a carriage house he'd refurbished with money from his books and lectures, the Center for Post-Marital Studies – an elaborate tax shelter, along with the foundation that raised funds to advance the work of the CPMS, which was primarily to pay its principal apostle – himself – to spread the word such as it was revealed to him. He'd kept pace with the rapidly expanding technologies of communications from bulk mail to blast fax, to email to website and blogosphere. Some nights, posting the latest news to the website, or linking a recent interview so his followers could listen in, he felt not a little like Paul writing epistles to the various churches. If, as that great circuit-rider wrote, it is better to marry than to burn, was it not much better still to divorce than to smolder? 'Exes', Adrian's favorite slogan held, 'you can't live with 'em and you can't shoot 'em. A little Good Riddance goes a long way.'

Walking in the moonlight across the gardened yard between his office in the carriage house and his residence, he would often consider how far he'd come in Findlay, Ohio, after all, from the little clapboard manse on Cory Street behind the church to this three-story palace with its towers and turrets, bay windows and balconies, its dozen cut-brick chimneys, lime-stone lintels and sills, its stained-glass transoms and fish-scale slates and fluted copper downspouts, its twelve-foot ceilings, tile baths, and mammoth basement with caverns and wine cellar, coal bins and cisterns, its dumbwaiter and dentil molds and third-floor ballroom, its nine species of hardwood floors and cabinets and crown moldings. And he would meditate on the apocryphal book of Sirach, its wisdoms on comfort and pleasure in 14:14, chapter and verse, to wit: 'Defraud not thyself of the good day, and let not the part of a good desire overpass thee.' He had come to admire about the Hebrews and Greeks their sense that this life might be as good as it gets, that whatever might be coming after this – Hades or Shades or heavenly mansions – mightn't be something to bank much on. Maybe it's much like the devil, he thought: the heaven you know is better than the one you don't. Adrian would look up into the moon's face, whatever there was of it, and offer thanks for the progress he had made since he'd been left by his wife and quietly exiled from St. Mark's Methodist, across the street and three blocks north, all those years ago. That local Methodists could not help but pass his place and might pause to wonder in their daily rounds if the mansions being prepared for them in heaven would ever be as sumptuous as the one their former associate pastor now occupied in Findlay was part of the good day of which Adrian would not defraud himself. Such sentiments he knew did not ennoble him but there they were and he could not deny them. The retinue of Mexican landscapers, housekeepers, and handymen required in every season, the steady traffic of visitors and conferees who would come for weeklong intensive residencies over which Adrian presided like a maharishi to the formerly married, the occasional news or documentary crew, the place's reputation for haute cuisine, wine tastings, harp and flute recitals, a growing collection of private art, book launches – these were all the stuff of local rumor and gossip. He had become in Findlay a man of parts, none entirely known. To Methodists and their united brethren, no less to the nonbelievers hereabouts, Adrian had become a local notable and celebrity. After pissing off the back porch into the thick beds of variegated hostas that bordered the property, he would enter the back door with a benediction, 'God bless all here and bless this house', pour himself a glass of something, and make his way upstairs to his private rooms.

In the years since *Riddance* was released, he'd written *The Good Riddance Workbook* and *Questions & Answers About Good Riddance*, thereby giving the trilogy his publisher said really would saturate the market. A coffee table book, provisionally

titled *Second Chances* and featuring the personal stories and
posed photographs of successfully divorced people from all over
the country, was in production. It showed them in their new
habitats and fashions, smiling knowingly, or looking healthy
and well and newly 'centered', preoccupied with lives of evident
merit and higher purpose. One of Adrian's devotees who did
architectural photography was doing the images while Adrian
was preparing some introductory text. The more that offers
came into the Center for PMS, the more he raised his fees for
speaking, which had the effect of making him seem worth that
much more, which brought, of course, more offers. He counted
it an irony, and a pleasant one, that he'd become, de facto, an
itinerant preacher – the calling he'd felt early and often in his
youth – albeit preaching a secularized gospel that was a hybrid
of pop psyche, warm fuzzies, personal witness, and cultural
study. That he homilized not from the pulpits of great cathe-
drals but from the lecterns of convention hotels struck him as
part of the Creator's plan for him. He'd stopped saying 'Gawd'
in the deeply reverential tone of his Methodist training and
taken rather to the user-friendly, guilt-free parlance of nature
and creation. It was, he told himself, more 'inclusive.' That he
traveled like a Wesleyan but was paid like a free-market capital-
ist filled him with a sense of this life's mysteries. Likewise, he'd
given up 'the Reverend' for simply 'Dr.' Adrian Littlefield for
the scholarly, vaguely medicinal ring that it added to his brief.
He had a D.D. mail order from one of the agencies that adver-
tised in clergy magazines and an honorary doctorate from his
alma mater, Ohio Wesleyan, where he'd given the commence-
ment speech the year after his book came out. He had done
postgraduate work at the Methodist Theological Seminary in
Delaware – a course of study he let lapse after the divorce. He

was certainly not the first to observe that the high priests of the current culture had secular rather than sacred credentials. Not lost on him either was the happy fact that divorcing, conventionally regarded as a failure, had been the essential key to his success. Though the scandal had cost him his job as the long-suffering and underpaid associate pastor at St. Mark's, as soon as his wife left him he became the tragically abandoned and heroically single father of two youngsters. Once the book came out, with excerpts published in *Redbook* and *Esquire*, interviews on public radio, profiles on prime-time network shows, he'd become a kind of local hero. He'd even gone to Chicago for a sit-down with Oprah, to chat and answer the audience questions, which appearance alone had accounted for a massive third printing of *Riddance* and an audio book.

When he found himself, as he often did, departing some posh hotel, with the hefty stipend cooling in his briefcase, the livery sedan idling at the curbside to take him to the plane, the appreciation of conventioneers ringing in his ears, and, as luck would occasionally have it, a woman waking in the bed upstairs to find him gone but not, he could convince himself, entirely forgotten, Adrian Littlefield's heart filled with thanksgiving for the failure of his marriage. All things, he told himself, work together toward some good. And the new life, such as he had come to know it, had restored to him some holy order, a sense of real purpose and calling and voice. If God was a practical joker, well then he would grin and bear it. He offered, in such moments, silent and abundant thanks and praise to Whoever Was In Charge Here, as he had come to call his Lord and Savior, the one he believed might still be out there, wherever, listening to his heart of hearts.

◆   ◆   ◆

IT WAS the National Association of Family Law Attorneys (NAFLA) annual meeting in Connecticut that brought him to the Foxwoods Casino – a high-stakes bingo parlor parlayed by the Mashantucket Pequot Tribal Nation into one of the most profitable gaming emporiums in the country. It rose out of the hilly forests between Norwich and the coast, like something out of Kubla Khan, its lights blazing in the darkness, a pleasure dome on the 'rez'.

'More than a hundred thousand an hour, twenty-four hours a day, three hundred and sixty-five days, et cetera, et cetera', the limo driver who met his flight in Hartford said, drawing out the syllables of the *et ceteras* for emphasis, 'that's net-net in profit. Every day. Pretty good revenge, eh? We gave them firewater and reservations, they give us Keno and the dollar slots. They don't call it wampum for nothing, eh!'

The shops and restaurants and conference center and hotel all played into the tribe's master plan – to disabuse as many of their former oppressors of as much money as possible in the most mindless way. It seemed a suitable locale for the divorce attorneys to hold their annual meeting. Dr. Littlefield was the keynote speaker. His fee was fifteen thousand, first-class travel, ground transport, premium lodging and meals. His books and videos sold briskly after his lectures. He signed them *Best wishes – A.L.*, and if the purchaser was a woman of a certain age and style he'd add, *every available benevolence*. He thought this sounded a literary chord, and while what he wrote was far from literary, he thought the pretence would do no harm. Also, it gave him time to ask some chatty questions.

'And what do you do?' he'd ask her flatly.

'Whatever it takes', or 'Well, that depends', some would flirt, whereas others would offer only 'mediation and depositions.'

In most cases he would fly into a venue the night before, check in, order a chicken salad from room service, watch a movie, and go to bed. He would be up early the next morning to walk, then ready himself for his standard forty-five-minute speech, fifteen minutes of Q&A and whatever it took to sign all the books. Then he'd collect the balance of his fee and make for the airport and the next venue.

But the NAFLA conference was in late July, in a resort casino near the sea in New England. He'd been going nonstop for most of the year and the pictures in the pre-registration packet looked inviting. Along with the predictable workshops on 'Custody Issues' and 'Grandparents' Rights' and 'Pre-and-Post-Marital Agreements', there was a 'Traditional Yankee Clambake' scheduled at Mystic Seaport, a golf outing, and 'A Day on Beautiful Block Island.' He'd never been to Block Island but he had kept a picture of the place in his imagination for years. The brochure photo of handsome couples assembled around fruity drinks, smiling from the wide porch of an elegant nineteenth-century hotel, caught his eye. He told the organizers he'd be staying for the entire conference, and while he wouldn't play golf with the attendees, he'd be happy to eat with them and wanted to take the trip to the island. They were happy to book him two more nights in the suite, knowing that their members would be pleased at the chance to visit with their keynote speaker.

◆   ◆   ◆

THE TOUR bus from Foxwoods to Point Judith took an hour. The boat from Point Judith to Block Island took another – thirteen miles across Block Island Sound from Galilee, Rhode Island, to the town of New Shoreham at the Old Harbor. Stepping aboard the car ferry *Anna C.*, Dr. Adrian Littlefield tried to imagine what crossing water must have added to the romance his former spouse must have felt en route to the first of her infidelities. He took a seat on the middle deck of the ferry among the conferees from NAFLA, who sat in a block in the first few rows of benches, careful to get an aisle seat for the escape he planned once the boat was on its way. They waited for cars and day-trippers to board, admiring the small fleet of fishing vessels in Point Judith. The *Enterprise* and *Lady Helen* and *Stormy Elizabeth* – it was not so much the names of vessels as the black riggings and booms and spools of netting that put him in mind of life's entanglements. He thought he might begin another series of books entitled *Life's Entanglements*. He took a notebook from his shirt pocket and wrote in it, *Life's Entanglements?* and underlined the entry.

'*Good Riddance* was a miracle for me! I have to tell you, Doctor . . .'

'Oh, thank you,' he smiled at the red-haired woman sitting next to him, 'that's very flattering.'

'No really, Doctor. It gave me permission to . . . I hope I'm not interrupting your . . .'

'No, no, not at all. I'm glad you liked it.'

'I mean before your book I never would have, you know, felt empowered.' She emphasized the middle syllable of 'em*pow*-ered' like she had 'per*mis*sion.'

'Yes, yes', Adrian said, and looked deeply into her blue eyes, trying to imagine what idiom from the lexicon of daytime talk shows she would give out with next, a scrutiny which the red-haired woman mistook for interest.

'Of course, there's so much baggage we had to let go of first, my ex and me, before we could, you know, grow up and grow apart, you know, together.'

Adrian nodded and smiled and stood and took her hand and held it meaningfully before looking about as a man does looking for the nearest toilet.

'Too much java', he said, to explain himself, and the man next to the red-haired woman pointed toward the rear of the ferryboat where they all had boarded.

'Head's at the back, Dr. Littlefield, we'll save your spot.'

Adrian smiled and made his move to the back of the boat just as it left Point Judith, and climbed the stairs to the open upper deck.

Block Island was the site of his former wife's first infidelity. He'd only ever seen it in pictures – photos that she'd brought home from her trip to New York that April, ostensibly to visit her friend Christina. 'I just need to get away from Findlay, and family and kids', she told him, 'just for a week, a little perker-upper. Christina has taken the time off of work, we're going to do girl things.' Clare was thirty-three at the time. They had a son and a daughter, ages eight and four. They'd been married almost twelve years. Her discontent was palpable.

'Oh, Ben invited us out to the island for the weekend', she told him when she returned from the week away, leaving him with the children and the house and his own work to manage. 'You remember Ben, don't you? Uncle Harold's friend? The artist, you know, Harold and Olive's neighbor. Christina and I ran into him in town, at his studio in SoHo, and he invited us out to the island for the weekend. We couldn't get theater tickets so we decided to go. Harold and Olive were going to come too but canceled at the last minute.'

Adrian remembered the determinedly plural references and the way it was supposed to work against his suspicions. And the supposed serendipity of it all, all very last-minute and carpe diem, nothing planned. Clare labored to make it all sound like happenstance, which of course made it all the more suspect. He rummaged through the photographs for any that included Christina. But there were none. There was Ben on the sailboat, manfully at the wheel, Ben in the kitchen, turning from the stove, Ben and Clare smiling from their places at a table on the porch of what looked like an old hotel. The table they were sitting at was set for two. Where, he wondered, was Christina? Where were Harold and Olive? Where were the photos of the 'girl things' they had done? Afraid of the answers, he never asked.

He'd met Ben once, the year they all drove East to visit Harold and Olive in Westchester. Harold was wealthy and worked in the city making investments for an insurance company. He had an office in Rockefeller Center and spent his lunchtimes all winter skating on the rink there and in the summer jogging through Central Park. All of Harold and Olive's friends were, like them, fiftyish, well-off, fit, and always grinning. None of them smoked. They all took vitamins. Everyone practiced some New Age regimen to guarantee a particular wellness. Ben was the next-door neighbor, 'heroically still married to his disabled wife' – an artist who lived on his earnings as an illustrator but was 'really just waiting to sell his marvelous oils.' He was tall and smooth-skinned and deeply tanned and his white hair and full beard made him look almost biblical. He'd done some covers for *Life* magazine and the *Saturday Evening Post*. Clare had confessed to Adrian the crush she'd had on Ben as a girl when visiting her uncle after her parents' divorce; Ben had made a fuss over her in some way she never elaborated, something to do with Rockefeller Center. He would have been in his thirties then and she'd always really 'felt really very special, you know, that he'd make such a fuss over a fifteen-year-old girl.'

Clare's own father had left when she was twelve, for reasons that were never made clear to her. One day he came in and said that he would always love her and then he left. Her mother looked a little wounded after that but never said a word about the divorce except 'I'm a one-man woman', which is why, Clare reasoned, her mother never remarried. After that they spent most summers and most Christmases with Uncle Harold and Aunt Olive.

All these years since, it all looked simple and predictable to Adrian now – the girl abandoned by her father looking for an older man's approval, attention, etc. etc. etc. – it was all embarrassingly usual, unremarkable in every way. A textbook case: she was driven, consciously or subconsciously, to replicate her father's rejection by sexual misconduct that would assure her husband's rejection. They had arranged their little off-season tryst while Adrian, the earnest ignoramus, stayed home with the kids and the church work, the reliable garden-variety cuckold and bumpkin, a brute if he raised objections, a wimp if he didn't, finished either way.

The *Anna C.* sounded its horn once and made its way out past the harbor's bars and seafood restaurants, out past the sunbathers waving from the shore, out past the rock pilings covered with cormorants, into the open water followed by maybe two dozen gulls which soared alongside the ferry for food tossed from passengers. Adrian Littlefield, seated between strangers on the long bench on the top deck, considered his fellow passengers from the isolation he had learned to wrap around himself in public transit. There were couples with children, college students in packs of various sizes, Asian tourists, and pairs of lovers, some obviously married, some obviously not. He watched as they grew more affectionate the further out from port the boat traveled. The touching and hugging and holding, and even kissing, grew more manifest as the mainland grew more distant. This he assigned to the crossing of water, the sense of privacy that passage to an island must add to the sense that all lovers share of being alone against the world and its elements.

One young couple, kissing like newlyweds, looked to Adrian like his son, Damien, and his girlfriend. They were handsome and serious, maybe bound for their honeymoon. The young woman snuggled into his half-embrace, safe and sound under his protection. The young man had Damien's wary eyes, keeping a reliable watch over everything, against the ever-present danger of the worst thing happening.

II

'LET'S GET Mom flowers', Damien would say, on the way home from grade school or St. Mark's day care. 'That'll surprise her.'

The things Adrian remembered after twenty years.

Adrian knew that Damien knew that all was not well between his mother and his father. And he knew the boy would keep trying to fix it.

It still stung him to think of the way his son, on those increasingly rare occasions when the family dined together, would rise to clear the table and offer to read his sister a bedtime story so 'you and Mom can go for a walk together around the neighborhood.'

The sweetness in the boy's eyes – his mother Clare's eyes, huge and blue – his sense that it could all be fixed with good behavior and the proper gesture, his hope in the face of a hopeless situation, still made Adrian Littlefield wince, these many years since, at the pain he knew had been inflicted on his son and daughter by the undoing of the marriage and the family. How his son had labored to keep them all together, to keep the little family unit intact, to keep the 'happily ever after' fiction going, still stung Adrian in his heart of hearts.

Damien was grown and out on his own now. He lectured in the Religious Studies program at a small private college in Michigan, happily distanced by nearly two decades from all that sadness, happily preoccupied with his own life's course, which included, apparently, a colleague who taught Old Testament Literature and who, Damien had told his father 'might be the one!' That the failure of his parents' marriage had not entirely disabused Damien of a sense of providence and kindly fates was a comfort to Adrian, who wondered at the resilience of the young, but remained vigilant for signs of permanent damage.

Damien called frequently and emailed often and drove down twice a year – for Father's Day and Christmas. He'd brought Jocelyn with him the last time he came, a pretty and pleasant woman, a few years older than Damien, not beautiful, but fetching, Adrian thought, diminutive and bookish, a perfect pastor's wife or professor's.

Adrian made his visits, too; whenever his lecture circuit took him anywhere near his daughter in Chicago or his son in Michigan, he'd add on a day to pay his call. They'd have dinner, see a movie or some local attraction. They had devised, if not any sense of a family 'home' – safe harbor, big extended family dinners, year-in, year-out traditions – nonetheless a kind of family life à la carte, keeping up contacts and appearances, juggling the reconstituted relations admirably.

Still, Adrian's remorse, his guilt for his part in it – the poor choice of spouse he had made, his failure to retain their mother's love, the remarkable sense of liberty once she'd gone, and the turn for the better his own life took once she had vacated their lives and premises – it all still netted out as sharp regret whenever he thought of his daughter, Sarah, named for the patriarch's wife, or his son, Damien, named for the saintly priest who'd served the lepers on Molokai; Damien, a beautiful, sad boy just gone eight, that awful summer all those years ago.

AT THE time, of course, it seemed so sudden; but in hindsight Adrian could see the turns in the journey that ended in their divorce. Clare had given up her household routines and enrolled in classes at the University of Findlay. It was the mid 1980s and she wanted to go into video production and shoot films that would get played on MTV, like Michael Jackson's *Thriller*, which she watched over and over and worked out to at her aerobics class in the morning; or documentaries about wage discrimination and spousal abuse, the urban poor and world hunger she would eventually sell to public TV. She was waging a war against the tummy and cellulite that had appeared on her body and which she blamed on her pregnancies. She went off in a sweatband and leg warmers and a leotard in the morning, then came home and showered and went off to school for the afternoons. Adrian took Damien to Lincoln Elementary and brought Sarah to the day care at St. Mark's Methodist, then picked Damien up after school and brought them home and made them supper. Clare let it be known that she'd been more or less duped by the culture into marriage and having babies. Adrian was part of the conspiracy – not willfully perhaps, not purposefully, but part of the conspiracy nonetheless – that sought to shackle Clare's life and prospects to these other lives. Damien and Sarah were part of the conspiracy too, needy as they were of so much attention. Like his father, Damien constantly strove to make Clare happy – he was an excellent third grader, he read avidly, drew colorful pictures of happy vistas. Sarah was a tidy preschooler, too young, Adrian convinced himself, to sense, as Damien sensed, the coming disaster.

In the end it was not Ben Walters, the aging artist back East Clare left them for, but a fellow student from her video production class whose family had money and Clare could imagine financing her own filmmaking. Ben Walters had only been a test – a springtime fling, to see if it could be done, if other men wanted her, if she could do it. The summer she eventually moved out, the summer after the late-spring tryst with Ben, she spent shifting her friendships from hers and Adrian's circle of young parents and church families to the younger, entirely hipper, vastly more imaginative group of undiscovered artists and photographers David Eason hung out with at the university. David dressed in black denim pants and black silk shirts and wore a wide-brimmed black hat and looked artistic. David had long fingers and long curly black hair and dreams of enrolling in NYU's photography school; and Clare thought they'd go off to New York together, live in SoHo, and be young forever, and interesting.

When it dawned on Adrian that his wife might be having an affair, after David Eason's name kept turning up in her monologues on life and school and her widening prospects, after the same sick knot began to tighten in his stomach that he remembered from the months before when she'd returned from her adventures on Block Island, when the phone bill kept turning up lengthy calls to a number he didn't recognize, always placed during hours when he was at the church, when she'd stopped coming to bed with him and making excuses for her changing schedule, when he could no longer account for the changes in her, he asked if she'd 'see someone' with him. A therapist or counselor, 'someone to talk to about saving the marriage' because, as he tried to explain to her, 'there are two little lives depending on us, to get this right and keep it together.' When she refused his suggestion about marriage counseling, he found someone he could talk to himself, to sort out his feelings of anger and fear. Eventually it was this therapist who diagnosed Clare in absentia as 'possibly a narcissist' and Adrian as 'possibly an enabler, a co-narcissist', a man who would never satisfy a narcissist's appetite for grandiosity, and the more he tried the more feckless he would seem to her and that for her part Clare was probably 'already psychologically divorced' from him. It was then that Adrian hired a private investigator to follow Clare around and take pictures and document her adulteries. Adrian believed it would help with the eventual proceedings and with the custody issues. And he thought he should have certainty, beyond reasonable doubt, before dropping a hammer he knew would do irreparable damage. He could imagine a life without Clare, but could simply not abide a life distant from his children's lives.

He got photos of Clare and David coming and going at hotels along I-75, tastefully north and south of Findlay, where only transients and other adulterers might be. There were detailed logs of their arrivals, departures, room numbers, dates and times. Adrian calculated that the average stay was 2.75 hours, which he tried to divide into foreplay, intercourse, and afterglow, and was bothered to find himself slightly aroused by these contemplations. After twelve years he felt he knew Clare's sexual repertoire – what she liked to do and have done to her – and the thought of her doing those things with someone else first enraged, then excited, then sickened, then saddened him. There were photos of them having dessert at a Cracker Barrel restaurant near the Lima exit. They looked like teenagers, sharing a piece of Boston cream pie, surrounded by booths full of old married couples, their forks hovering over the pie on the plate, nearly touching, their eyes fixed deeply on each other's eyes. There was a background workup on David Eason, who, except for the fact that he still lived with his parents at age twenty-nine, in the carriage house of one of the great mansions on Sandusky Street, and had been hospitalized once for an unspecified nervous disorder, seemed unremarkable in every way. A month or so into their affair, midway through the spring semester, Clare and David planned a romantic weekend at a boutique hotel in Cincinnati. Clare had told Adrian she was going to film a short movie about the Anderson Ferry that brought cars back and forth across the Ohio River, to fulfill requirements for her video arts class.

'It's the last of the old ferryboats on the Ohio – since 1817! There's a whole crew of us going, production and sound, camera and lighting, we're going to submit it to short film competitions. We'll be staying in dorm rooms at Mount St. Joseph. There are no phones. I'm riding with the other camera operator.' Clare had her story perfectly constructed. Adrian had smiled agreeably, and nodded and said nothing except that he'd watch the kids. While she packed a small bag, he called his detective.

That evening, after Clare went off waving from David Eason's Toyota van, Adrian took Sarah and Damien out to St. Michael the Archangel's for the annual parish fair and let them ride the rides and eat cotton candy and sit under the big tent eating spaghetti and meatballs with the Catholics. He walked with them among the booths of crafts and white elephants and children's games and bought them both chances at ringtoss and beanbags. He could not resist the urge to spoil them with diversions and easy pleasures. He peeked into the casino tent with blackjack tables and roulette wheels and tables of bingo games and wondered at the way these otherwise devout people would wallow in sin for a worthy cause. Whereas the Baptists had bake sales and the Methodists did Christmas bazaars, the Episcopalians favored crafts and antiques sales and the Presbyterians were forever doing dinners and teas to raise money for their various causes, there was something to envy in the way these Poles and Germans, Italian and Irish Catholics would indulge their nearly pagan appetites to put some money in the priests' pension fund or a new roof on the rectory or construct a bell tower to sound the angelus all over town. Food and drink and dance and games of chance – St. Michael the Archangel's parish fair had become the biggest and best of the churchy entertainments in Findlay, the opening of the summer season, and folks from all over Hamilton County came.

Adrian sat at a long table littered with half-empty plastic

cups of beer and soda, in the main tent where a band was playing. He gave Damien a roll of tickets for rides and games and told him to hold his sister's hand. He sipped a Coca-Cola and looked at his watch to figure how far south Clare was by now. An accordion and clarinet wheezed between drumbeats from the bandstand at the end of the tent and Adrian found himself fixed on the long-married couples – bald men with plump bellies and women half again their marriage weight, still holding one another, after thirty or forty years, through waltzes and polkas, a little tipsy with the beer, the press of co-religionists and the humid evening air, like figures out of a Flemish painting, all knees and elbows and red faces sweltering under the canvas and party lights, circling in this rollicking dance.

'How you keeping, Adrian? Good of you to come.'

The priest startled Adrian from his contemplations.

'Oh, yes, yes, Francis, fine. And how are you? This extrava-ganza gets bigger every year!'

'First full convergence since the sixteenth century! You wanna raffle ticket?'

Adrian was still catching up to the priest's conversation.

'Convergence? Raffle?'

'Yep, first time since the Council of Trent that Friday the thirteenth and the full moon in June fall on the same day – should be lucky. First prize is a trip to Cancún for two. Clare would like that, Adrian. What say ye?'

The priest could sell anything, Adrian thought, especially in his slightly manic, larger-than-life incarnation as Father Francis Assisi Concannon, priest of God – half huckster, half holy man – the six-foot-four-inch lumbering frame clad in a Hawaiian shirt and Bermuda shorts, one fist full of dollars and another full of raffle tickets. Adrian fished five dollars from his pocket and handed it over.

'How many will that buy?'

'Only one, but it's all you'll need, bucko!'

Adrian and the priest had been friends for ten years since they'd both come to Findlay, fresh from their separate educations and appointments. The one and only meeting of the Findlay Ministerial Association, now defunct, had been held at St. Mark's Methodist. They played racquetball together, took in a movie from time to time, commiserated over parish politics and their bishops, and traded titles of books to read. Father Concannon favored Irish poets while Reverend Littlefield preferred spiritual guides and homiletics. *The Collected Poems of William Butler Yeats* got traded for *The Best of Robert Ingersoll*. Beckett got traded for Friderich Büchner. Every so often they'd go to dinner in the next town over, where no one knew them and they could be free of the scrutiny of parishioner and congregant.

'And where's the beautiful Mrs. Littlefield on such a fine moon and June and spooning evening?' The priest loved the sound of the pursed vowels in his mouth second only to the sound of his own voice. He pressed a ticket and pencil on the table for Adrian to fill out.

'She's gone to Cincinnati, to Mount St. Joseph.'

'Jaysus, Adrian, she's gone and joined the convent on ye – the nuns will rob you, man.'

Mount St. Joseph was one of the many holdings of the Sisters of Charity in Cincinnati – a four-year school for good Catholic girls, a fraction of whom would get a calling and join the order after graduation.

Adrian scribbled his name and phone number on the ticket

stub, tore off his portion, and gave the book of tickets back to the priest.

'She's gone past the point where the nuns would take her, Frank.'

Adrian wondered if the priest could hear more than small talk in what he'd said, the way he'd said it, and there was this sudden panic that he'd have to explain, to everyone – his parents and children, his senior pastor and his congregation, his neighbors and friends, old and new, the lawyers and taxman, God in heaven, everyone, everyone would know – that he had failed as a husband and father and head of the household; he had failed to keep his marriage intact, he had failed to keep his wife happy and satisfied and at home with her family where she belonged. Because he knew at the moment she was riding southbound with her new lover, David Eason, on I-75, maybe indulging in a little highway sex, his hand in her panties, her face in his lap, the reckless pleasure of it. He figured they were well south of Dayton now. Adrian knew he'd have to account to everyone but he just didn't want to do it now and so he smiled into the priest's inquisitive gaze.

'A film project, Francis, something for school.'

ADRIAN'S WIFE and her new lover had dinner on Mount Adams, in a small Italian restaurant, Guido's on the Hill, then strolled among the boutiques and galleries, then went to their room at the Cincinnatian and reappeared the following morning, when, hand in hand, they were photographed leaving the hotel together, each with their cameras and equipment bags. They drove out River Road, along the north shore of the Ohio to the southwest, and were photographed photographing

Anderson's Ferry, no doubt to supply some bit of alibi. They even rode it across the Ohio to the Kentucky shore, then back again. The photo of the ferry disappearing into the sunlit fog with the hills barely visible and half a dozen cars lined up on deck was almost artistic. Then they drove up Anderson Ferry Road to Delhi Road, where Adrian's detective took a photo of David taking a photo of Clare, posing among the summer semester students, at the door to one of the dorms, Clare trying her best to be 'one of the girls' though she was more than a decade older than them. Then they returned to the hotel and window-shopped downtown. She bought him a straw boater at Batsakes hat shop. He bought her flowers. It was all in the report. They returned to their room for their second night of bliss, new lovers in early June, carefree in a not-too-distant city.

Adrian was not proud of the fact that he'd hired DiBardino to spy on Clare, but he figured he really had to have proof, not only for the eventual proceedings, but for himself, before he could call an attorney from outside the congregation, have him file for divorce and an 'ex parte' order granting custody of 'the minor children' to him and possession of the marital home pending the outcome of the proceedings. He really had to know. He was not proud of the fact that he'd talked to an attorney who'd given him the number for the private eye and told him how to get the goods on Clare.

'What you want is chapter and verse, open-and-shut, a slam dunk. Play for keeps, Reverend, play to win it', the attorney told him. He said he'd need three thousand up front and would bill him for the balance, if there was any more. He promised discretion and anonymity.

It was early Sunday afternoon, after the eleven o'clock

service to which he always took his children and at which he preached, every other week, when DiBardino brought him the file and the photos. Reading it was like working a rotten tooth loose, the dull ache sharpening, then subsiding, then sharpening again, the nerve exposed, then numbing inexplicably.

It was the sentence in the report that read, 'Subjects were observed embracing in front of a church on Mount Adams', that finished it for him. He knew that she had taken her new lover there because it was where Adrian had taken her the night he had proposed to her almost a dozen years before. They'd had dinner at the Rookwood Pottery and walked up to Immaculata Church on the highest point of Cincinnati's seven hills. Adrian had planned this part. They'd walked up Guido Street to where it dead-ended in the small front courtyard of the church, surrounded by cast-iron fencing and overlooking the city. They had looked down on the wide turn of the Ohio River, and the city with its bridges, and the southwestern expanse of Kentucky and America, and pledged their love and planned their future there. They'd driven down from Delaware, where he was finishing his studies at Methodist Theological and she was a student at Ohio Wesleyan. They'd spent the day walking around Eden Park among the gardens and observatories. It was late summer and Clare was the golden girl of his dreams with whom he'd had sex maybe a half a dozen times since the night she came to him, to the flat he'd rented off campus, and kissed him and let her clothes be taken off of her. Though neither of them were virgins, neither was really experienced either. They were, in his memory of it, innocents. It was in front of the church atop Mount Adams he had taken from his pocket the quarter-karat diamond ring his mother had helped him buy the weekend before and he pressed it into her palm and said he wanted to be married to her and to live with her forever and to build a future with her and would she be his wife? She said nothing at first, only slipped the ring on her finger, kissed him deeply and pressed her head against his chest, sighed and said of course she would. 'My darling', she called him, 'of course.' In his memory of it, they seemed in love.

It was, in Adrian's heart, the place they were truly pledged, truly promised to one another, truly wed. In the early years of their marriage, when he wondered whether they were going to make it, it was that place, that moment, and its nearly cinematic replay in his memory that always convinced him they were meant for one another. And it was the wash of moonlight through the window of the Holiday Inn in downtown Cincinnati, which shone on Clare's bare shoulders as she knelt over his outstretched body that night, that still illumined his recollection of their sex, in slow motion, like a silent film – how she slowly bent to kiss him, letting her mouth with its warmth and quickened breathing work its way up and down his body, her hands so smooth, her arms outstretched, touching at once his right temple and his eyelids and his inner thighs, then taking him slowly into her mouth, hushing with the fingers of her left hand the catch of his breath, then in her own time, when he could not imagine any greater ecstasy, straddling him, taking him into herself – this was the consummation of their love, silver in every former remembrance, transcendent and sacramental, anointed, bathed in light, and now, now gone terribly, irretrievably dark.

That she would share their places with someone else seemed a more intimate betrayal than even sex. He called the attorney; he wept giving their particulars; full names, birth dates, date of marriage; the papers would be filed in the morning. She was served as she left her class with David Monday night. Adrian had left on Sunday afternoon and taken the children to visit his parents in Grand Rapids. He left a manila envelope on their bed, with photos of her and David coming and going from their assorted rendezvous and a note that told her he had 'chapter and verse' on her 'film project' and would use them against her if she contested anything. It would be a 'slam dunk'. She was to move out. 'Now.' He underlined the word. He included a check for five thousand dollars which he'd borrowed from the same church elder who'd loaned him the retainer for the attorney. She could use that to get set up in her 'new life'. She could keep the diamond ring, take anything she regarded as hers, and get out. He would contact the Western Ohio Conference of the UMC to find out whatever paltry amount had accrued to his pension fund and insurance account. If it was more than the five thousand, he'd pay her the difference. If it was less, she could keep the change. He wanted no fiscal entanglements between them. He would, he assured her, never keep the children from her, neither would he allow her to take them with her wherever it was she saw herself going. On this point Adrian was fairly certain that she would not put up much of a fight because what she really wanted was to travel light, free of encumbrances, into a new life with a new man off to New York where her truly artistic self would surface once the dull weight of husband and household and maternity had been lifted from her. He offered her, in this manila envelope, a package deal – freedom, some finances, and a permanent if à la carte relationship with her children, in trade for her getting out and letting everyone settle into the lives they would lead without her. Adrian, of course, had had the counsel of his attorney, who told him it would all go much better for him and for his children if there were truly no hope of reconciliation, if he could get Clare to move out of the 'marital home'. The photos, the check, the promises of freedom and a future of 'quality time' with her children, and the not-entirely-articulated but none-too-hidden threat of embarrassment, Adrian figured would be enough.

'Ohio is a no-fault state,' his attorney had told him, 'but when it comes to the division of property and the custody of minor children, who is at fault still matters to judges and jury panels.' Adrian had said as much in his note, which he paper-clipped to the photos and the check.

Over and over he had read the portions from the Gospel of Matthew – in the fifth chapter and the nineteenth – which held, 'Whosoever shall put away his wife, except it be for fornication, committeth adultery'. He read the same text in a different translation which replaced 'fornication' with 'marital infidelity'. He had, he assured himself, the perfect right to put Clare away, to save his children from her craziness, to free himself from this overwhelming pain.

In the end, of course, she moved out, not because of his threats but because of himself, and the dull life with him she no longer wanted and could no longer endure. She moved out because that's exactly what she wanted to do and Clare could be counted on to do what she wanted.

When Adrian and Damien and Sarah came home that Tuesday in the middle of June, to the house they had all shared on the corner of South Cory Street and Lima Avenue, some blocks south of the river that flowed through Findlay, Clare and her things were unmistakably gone. She had moved out, into an apartment on the other side of Findlay. She told the children she would always love them and would be coming back for them as soon as she got herself established.

'Everything is going to be really terrific! You're going to love New York! There's so much to see and do there. Not like "*Finally,* Ohio" – wait and see!' She'd come back for the last bits and pieces of her things. The white Toyota van was idling at the curb with the back doors open for Clare to pitch in garbage bags full of her clothes and linens.

They kept nodding and smiling and weeping and hugging her, their little hands and faces holding and searching and wondering why this was all happening and why couldn't she stay with them and be their mother and she would always be their mother no matter what and someday she was sure they'd understand and Adrian went into the house and vomited, because he felt so helpless, so totally lost in the tears of things, so angry and heart-rent and utterly helpless, and their mother's voice trailing off as she left them on the porch waving and sobbing and jumped in the van with her lover and drove off into the future. Adrian stood looking out of the screen door at the small figures of his children on the porch – all of this happening in slow motion now – as the van disappeared, and they raised their little hands and waved, and waved, and waved.

No remembrance of these events was free of the guilt Adrian still felt for the damage done his son and daughter, his complicity in its infliction.

Now what he could remember was the creak of the spring on the screen door as he pushed it open, and held it open and said, Come in now, and how the two of them turned, limp from the waving and weeping, and how Damien took his sister Sarah's hand and brought her back inside their suddenly and terribly broken home.

This was the moment, these many years since, that Adrian Littlefield could never forgive himself for – for failing his darling son and precious daughter so profoundly, for doing them such unspeakable damage by failing to keep their mother home, the marriage together, the household intact, life as they had come to know it safe and warm and blessed with abundant love. He couldn't protect his children from this hurt. His wife, their mother, had just driven off with her new lover, in a white van, leaving them all fixed and wriggling in the here and now without a clue as to what the future would hold. And as much as his heart hurt for his children's damage, standing at the kitchen counter buttering bread to make them grilled cheese sandwiches, and pouring out three matching glasses of milk, and cutting up a green apple into six little wedges, and placing this meal before them, and holding their tiny hands saying 'Let us pray', and hearing their little voices give out with the accustomed grace, to wit: 'God is great, God is good . . .' some corner of his broken, brooding heart quickened with the hope that his own life and times might just have gotten better, easier, simpler, saner somehow. Good riddance, he did not say out loud, while they ate their sandwiches wordlessly, but he said it nonetheless, good riddance, indeed.

That night he tucked them into bed and said their prayers with them, including the part about God blessing 'Mommy and Daddy and Gramma and Grandpa and all the children in the world who don't have homes' and promised that everything was going to be all right and they'd go tomorrow for Vacation Bible Camp. Then he sat out on the porch, watching the darkness tighten around the neighborhood and the bats circling out of the trees up and down the street and sipped from a tumbler of whiskey he'd taken to pouring himself, at the suggestion of the same church elder who'd loaned him money. 'It'll help you sleep', is what he'd said.

And as often happened then and now, something out of Scriptures came to mind. *May your fountain be blessed, and may you rejoice in the wife of your youth. A loving doe, a graceful deer – may her breasts satisfy you always, may you ever be captivated by her love. Why be captivated, my son, by an adulteress?* Adrian remembered this reading from their wedding. He had chosen it from Proverbs, Chapter 5, as a reminder of the gifts of fidelity. Of course, he chose it as a warning against mannish misconduct – the biblical and still-conventional wisdom which assigned to men brute passions and moral weakness and more or less assumed that he would stray while she, the 'loving doe' and 'graceful deer' would remain true and unblemished by temptation. Now he read it as a cruel twist of his cuckolding, that even the Scriptures seemed to mock him. He had been happy enough, satisfied, captivated by her love, such as he'd known it, captivated by an adulteress, after all.

His fountain seemed blighted, the wife of his youth banished. The loving doe and graceful deer she'd seemed for years now seemed a snarling bitch; her breasts gone dry, now satisfying David Eason, the silly fuck, captivated by an adulteress with stretch marks, hemorrhoids, more wear and tear than he might've imagined. Adrian gulped the bourbon. It made his eyes water. The taste of it, deliciously sinful for a Methodist, burned his tongue and the back of his throat and made him feel suddenly wonderful, capable, incredibly released, as if the whole of this disaster might be managed. But at night he wept.

WHEN HE woke in the morning, dry-mouthed, slightly hungover, but the children alive and sleeping soundly and himself alive and the sky remarkably not fallen, it seemed to Adrian they might all survive, the wife of his youth's departure not-withstanding. He pulled the photos DiBardino had given him from out of the large manila envelope marked CONFIDENTIAL and carefully tore them all to shreds, all but the one of Anderson's Ferry, its paddle wheels flanking its barge of cars, its fog lights beaming from above the pilot's cabin – *Boone No. 7 Port of Cincinnati* – easing out from shore into the crosscurrents of the river, its masts and antennae turning and tuned in, the dense fog lifting off the water. That one Adrian Littlefield kept.

III

WHEN BLOCK Island came into view, he could see the tall sand cliffs, the green headlands, and the litter of sailing boats. From the dock in Old Harbor, Block Island seemed to Adrian like a postcard of the upmarket Yankee resort – huge painted Victorian hotels overlooking the harbor with red, white, and blue buntings hanging from their broad verandas, sloops and schooners and power yachts scattered around the seafront, brightly painted shop fronts done up for the season, and an abundance of cedar-shingled housing, gray-ing but not particularly aged. Everywhere there were tanned and happy people in shorts and sandals and designer eyewear going about no particular business. There were bicycles and mopeds and cars for hire. The dockside was busy with day trippers and courtesy vans from the various hotels meeting their guests. There were grandparents there to welcome their visiting families and the predictable vignettes of arrival and departure that are all the business of ports of call. Adrian Littlefield waited while the other passengers disembarked. The organizer from the National Association of Family Law Attorneys, holding her clipboard and smiling widely, was reminding the attorneys to 'be back for the four o'clock ferry! We have the installation of officers ball tonight at Foxwoods!' This gave the group five hours to tour the island, maybe take a swim, maybe browse the shops for souvenirs. Adrian waited for the rest to leave. He wanted to do his tour alone. He walked through the town, looking over the offerings in store windows, admiring the lithe bodies of women in beachwear, looking into the faces of men. At the top of the Main Street where the road turned sharply left, he came to the National Hotel. It looked familiar to him. He climbed the front steps and took a seat on the long porch where lunch was being served. He ordered iced tea and, from the list of appetizers, steamers in drawn butter, a cup of seafood chowder, and bruschetta. A little taste of everything, he thought. He had a good view of the harbor and the foot traffic coming and going along the Main Street front.

There were fathers with cell phones, their teenagers on holidays with their noncustodial parents – subversive daughters being courted by their new stepmothers, young boys bristling at the new men in their mothers' lives. There were young couples traveling *en famille*, with toddlers and infants and bored preteens.

He could see in the faces of the young husbands the fear he had felt in himself at that age, that he'd be overwhelmed at any minute by the duties and expenses and decisions.

He could see in the faces of their wives the worry and regret and second-guessing. How, they seemed to be asking themselves, had they gotten themselves into this predicament? They had been young and footloose and passionate and now they were homebound and bored and fatigued by motherhood and family life. They had been creative and well-read and interesting. Now they were dull, bored, vexed by the daylong needs of their offspring.

Adrian tried to reckon the ones who would make it and the ones who wouldn't. He tried to guess, by something in the way they walked or interacted, which of the children for whom this would be the last real family vacation. In the future there would be other configurations of adults and siblings in their lives. Partners, companions, significant others, spousal equivalents, stepparents, stepsisters, half brothers. But for many this would be the last vacation where mother and father shared the same time of their lives.

He was aware of a kind of psychic wince that always registered wrongly as a smile on his face whenever he looked at children and thought of his own children's pain, courageously borne in the years after their mother left. Of course, there was nothing he could do. Still he suffered a kind of survivor's guilt that what had been the best change in his life and the lightning rod of his success had hobbled his son and daughter somehow, in ways he sensed but could not measure. He had been a good parent and a good provider but he had not loved their mother. And now, in their young adulthood, he could see in the lives of his son and daughter that essential mistrust of their own hearts, a wariness about the love of others that made it difficult for them to form intimate attachments. He looked for early signals of such things in the manner and conduct of the children passing by.

He could see as well the older men eyeing the younger women and felt a quiet kinship with them. Adrian had counted it among the blessings of age that the abundance of women he found attractive was ever broadening, even as his sexual prowess began to falter. The older he got the more and younger women there were to look at. Their beauty, at every age, took more of his breath away than it had when he was a much younger man.

He'd quit begrudging Clare her infidelities. The sense of sexual betrayal had been replaced by an understanding of it as a failure of honesty. Not that she'd had sex with Ben or David or whomever else, but that she'd not been forthright with Adrian. He could forgive her giving into an urgency of desire, but did not forgive her hiding it from him. Nor could he much blame Ben for taking advantage of the situation. They were the necessary precipitators or necessary events – an evolution, a natural elaboration of an order whereby the universe of love and attachment purges itself of anomalies. A man of fifty-something – as Adrian was now, as Ben had been then – could not easily resist the proffered affections of a woman twenty years his junior. Nor could a woman unhappy in her home life, tired of small towns and small children, bored by her husband's regular and routine affections, worried over the pressing and passage of time, be expected to travel in the off-season with a handsome artist to a distant island, to sail and walk deserted beaches and talk over dinner, idling away the remains of the day, and not offer her body to him. Especially when he had made a fuss over her as a girl. It was only natural for a woman at a loose end and a man in his fifties to fall into a fitful consortium should the occasion arise.

Adrian Littlefield had himself made a habit of confirming this in the years since, every chance he got, which was mostly at conventions such as the one he was currently hired to hold forth to. Attended as they always were by more than a few of the recently divorced, or recently traded in for a younger, fresher model, or recently disappointed in love or perennially discontented with life, these professional conferences provided cover for those occasions when the sexually rejected might reconfirm their sexiness. Chief among the obligations – Adrian knew this from his own experience – of every newly divorced man and woman was to demonstrate that it was not a sexual dysfunction that occasioned the breakup. As the keynoter and visiting expert at these confabs and conventions, Adrian was often the focus of much of the free-floating, unattached, ready, willing, and able sexual energy of the registrants, a number of whom, without fail, would make known in the usual ways to Adrian their availability for more intimate conversations on related themes. He was possessed, after all, of a certain celebrity in these circles. He was famously single, well-spoken, well-dressed, well-paid, and the center of an hour or two hours' attention during which he would motivate, inspire, entertain, inform, and uplift his listeners. To be gracious, charming, self-effacing was easier after a standing ovation, handsome payment, and a line of supplicants waiting for a signature on a book that bore his face and name on the cover. He had no less an appetite for a stranger's affections than any man or woman did. And while he sometimes missed the predictable lovemaking of the married life, he found it hard to count as anything but good fortune that the years since the dissolution of his marriage had been characterized by sexual encounters more abundant if more distant, more passionate if less precise, hungrier if less often sated, more memorable if often nameless. If each partner in these arrangements felt a little 'used', it was, to him and to no few of the women he had

had sex with, still pleasant enough. That bodies could pleasure and could be pleasured, free of social, emotional, or intellectual encumbrances, seemed to Adrian a good and wholesome thing. And he made it his mission to attend to his partner in ways that would overwhelm whatever residual regret she might otherwise attach to the 'one-night stand'. With several of these women he had maintained an ongoing correspondence, some of which had ended sooner, some later, and some of which remained pleasant and unpredictable addenda to his professional life. Sometimes he would invite one of them to join him on an extended speaking tour. They would spend a week, or maybe two weeks, together. They'd begin to behave like real companions. He'd remember how she drank her coffee and order room service accordingly. She'd pack and unpack his things between hotels. Each would pretend an intimacy they both knew did not, and likely would never, really exist. They would tell each other secrets over dinner. It warmed something in Adrian he could never quite identify. Getting to know someone after having sex with them was a reversal of the usual arrangement by which the business of intimacy was in the main conducted, but for a variety of reasons, it appealed to him. The flesh, Adrian sometimes pointed out in his workshops, is far less particular than the heart or the mind when it comes to finding 'suitable' partners. Sex between people who might not otherwise find anything to admire about one another could be quite, well, satisfactory, especially on a time-fixed basis. Whereas, he would likewise observe, there were people who could be attracted in every possible way, intimate in all ways in the conduct of their lives together, but sexually uninspired. These were but a few among the many mysteries his programs dealt with. And Adrian had seen in the faces of the registrants at Foxwoods, in the small talk of the NAFLA conferees, in the body language of their pairings and couplings and comminglings at the welcome reception the night before, chitchatting with wines and finger foods, the men in their best business-casual attire, the women wanting to look professional but sexy – he had seen it all – the whole register of human want and willingness and desire.

Adrian could see it now, watching from the long porch of the National Hotel, the parade of suffering humankind, bearing their various histories and fears of missed chances and discontents along the esplanade, the mercilessly sunlit day unfolding around them; it was inevitable. 'The story of love', as he often told his audience, 'to quote Professor Bowlby, is told in three volumes: Attachment, Separation, and Loss.' Or if the time allowed only a thumbnail version, 'Love', he would say, quoting Roy Orbison, 'hurts.'

'No pair of words ever added up to more truth than that!' Adrian would often close his keynotes with the observation.

'Boudleaux Bryant wrote it. Roy Orbison sang it. Everyone in the room here knows it – *Love hurts!* We ante up, we go all in, we play the cards we're dealt as best we can, and still it comes down to a simple two-word arithmetic, this fact of life: *Shit happens, Jesus wept, Life sucks, Love hurts.* And yet we keep on playing for keeps because *Love heals, love sings, love haunts, love holds, love gives, love takes, love warms, love knows, love waits, love weeps, love laughs, love lives, love lasts, God is love and love never ends.* This litany of love, for which Adrian had become well-known, always signaled the end of his speech. He would let the last words settle in the air, careful to keep his gaze fixed above their heads, off in the distance beyond the back of the room, then step back from the lectern, let his hands fall to his side and his head bow slightly, which never failed to bring on the first round of applause. 'Thank you' he would say, holding his hands to his heart as the applause grew louder. 'Thank you, thank you . . . you are so very kind . . .' It would bring them to their feet. He would bow again.

ADRIAN LITTLEFIELD looked down the long porch of the National Hotel and tried to envision his ex-wife Clare in her thirties seated at one of these tables with her old artist Ben, wizened and hirsute, each of them pleased with what they had just accomplished by getting sufficiently free of life's entanglements to arrive here on the island together, off-season, unencumbered. Like Ben's wife, Adrian and the children had been jettisoned, thrown overboard to the fish or gulls, somewhere en route between the mainland and island. How knowingly they must have smiled at one another, how free of any moral vexation, how entitled they surely must have felt to their mutual lapses of faith. Or maybe not. Maybe there was some whiff of regret. How could he ever know? How, of course, could Findlay, Ohio, flat and landlocked, compete with an island in the ocean? How could an associate pastor compete with a true artist or a sickly, sexless, disabled wife back in Westchester – how could she compete with a young and eager and interested girl?

ADRIAN PICKED at the elements of his meal. He wasn't as hungry as he'd thought. He asked for the bill, left a large gratuity, and asked the waitress for another cup of coffee and a local phone book.

IV

Father francis Assisi Concannon phoned the Reverend Adrian Littlefield and told him to be ready at five o'clock.

'I can't make it, Francis. I've got kids to watch.'

'I'm bringing a sitter. We need a night out.'

'No really, Francis, I really can't.'

'Never cross a priest, Adrian. It's bad karma. See you at five.'

Word about the marital woes of the associate pastor at Findlay's St. Mark's Methodist Church had gotten round all over that part of Ohio. If bad news travels fast, Adrian observed, news involving the private lives of the reverend clergy moved like wildfire. *And the tongue is a fire*, he recalled from the Letter of James. *The tongue is set among our members as a world of iniquity; it stains the whole body, sets on fire the cycle of nature, as is itself set on fire by hell.*

A tongue among my members would be just the thing, he thought, then tried to turn his thoughts to godly themes.

'The people who know you know you', his father had told him when Adrian had shared his worry over the gossip that was circulating about his wife leaving him. 'And those who don't, don't care.' But Adrian knew that people were talking. Clare had spent a few weeks in an apartment on the north end of Findlay, then moved to Bowling Green, then eastward on to Cleveland.

She kept giving Damien new phone numbers which the boy

would sit repeating to himself until he had them memorized. To watch his son, just gone eight years old, holding the slip of paper, quizzing himself and his little sister Sarah on their mother's new numbers hurt Adrian and angered him.

From the same mouth come blessing and cursing. Does a spring pour forth from the same opening both fresh and brackish water? Whenever he heard some strand of a rumor about his predicament, he renewed his vow to keep silent rather than add his own fiery tongue – *a restless evil full of deadly poison* – to the general conflagration.

Oh, to put my tongue to better use, he thought, at the altar of some good woman's pleasure . . . then caught himself again and tried to budge his brain from the parts of women.

Whether it was coincidence, correlation, or cause and effect, soon after Clare Littlefield moved out of the manse, her cuckolded husband's sermons began to draw more listeners to church. Adrian thought it was mostly the spectacle of a churchman writhing in such worldly pain that packed the pews. *Not many of you should become teachers,* James the brother of Jesus advised, *for you know that we who teach will be judged with greater strictness.*

Folks from as far off as Fostoria and Columbus Grove, Bowling Green and Bucyrus would show up for the eleven o'clock services on the every other Sundays Adrian preached. Even his Wednesday night Bible Study, formerly a lackluster assembly of elders and widows, suddenly had new faces, younger faces, and more females than ever before. His former custom of preparing typed sermons, two minutes a page, eight pages per service of carefully constructed remarks on some biblical principle, gave way to a much looser, catch-as-catch-can delivery. This owed to the necessities of his newly single life

as the custodial parent of two young children. He hadn't the
time proper preparation takes, to study the readings from the
Lectionary, and find some way to connect those dots.

In the years of his marriage he'd spend every other Saturday night in his office at St. Mark's, preparing his sermon for
the following morning. He liked to think of members of the
congregation, driving up and down South Main at all hours,
returning from boozy dinners, late movies, the shift change at
Cooper Tires, God knows what assignations – how they would
see the lights blazing from his basement office and know he was
hard at the Lord's work late at night.

'You were burning the midnight oil again', someone would
always say, shaking his hand after Sunday services. Adrian
thought it was a good thing to be known for. The Reverend
Hinkston had a fairly comprehensive library, which he had
generously opened to Adrian. It had volumes of old sermons,
church histories, homiletic guides, and toastmaster's resources.
A formula for his homilies had emerged, by which he sought
to speak to his entire flock, young and old, devout and back-
sliding, male and female, country and townie, educated and
simple. He would pick out a couple of homey anecdotes with an
evident lesson, maybe a verse from Helen Steiner Rice for the
blue hairs, some folksy jokes, and something from the current
music, 'a little bit country, a little bit rock and roll', to keep the
younger crowd alert. To these he would add something from
the day's Scripture readings and tie them all together seam-
lessly, like the papers he wrote in seminary – five paragraphs,
compare and contrast, beginning, middle, and end – methodical. Thus, Jesus would be our 'bridge over troubled waters' and
Moses was an example of 'knowing when to fold and knowing
when to hold them'.

He'd type them up with double spacing and wide margins for notes he might add in longhand afterward, shifting those points he most wanted to stress into capital letters and underlining things he might want to repeat. The old Underwood his father gave him had given way to an Olympia Electronic and then to an IBM Selectric. He would go into the darkened sanctuary and test his delivery in the vaulted acoustics of the worship space. 'My brothers and sisters in Christ Jesus Arisen', he would always open. He would listen for the echo of his own voice off the stone walls and open the articulation of the words to allow for this amplification. 'Amen and Amen', he would almost always close, in a style borrowed from a TV preacher he'd seen as a boy who would heal people by the laying on of hands. And though his sermons were, in their printed versions, carefully wrought and often very readable, and though he kept copies for his pastoral archives, the homilies he labored over were as enthusiastically ignored and as politely disregarded by his congregants as the Reverend Hinkston's famous 'three points and a poem' snorers. Regardless of what it was he was saying, he could effect no manifest change in the congregants' response. The smilers kept smiling, the nodders kept nodding, the sighers kept sighing, the dozers kept getting elbowed by their wives. 'Uplifting message this morning', Mrs. Melzer would always say, shaking his hand and pressing the handkerchief to her nostrils. 'Covered all the bases today, Reverend', Clark Waters, the head of the DPW would say without fail. 'A blessing, a blessing, words from the heart', the breathless Donna Montgomery would always own, holding her right hand over her bosom and offering her left hand for Adrian to take in the kind of straight-armed feint he always associated with characters from a Tennessee Williams play. He would assume his place at the back doors of the church while half of the congregants made for the parking lot and the other half made for the fellowship hall where coffee and donuts and cookies were served.

Whatever the response, Adrian counted himself blessed to have anyone listening at all. So many churches had lost members to the growing horde of radio and TV preachers – Swaggart and the Bakkers, Jerry Falwell and Pat Robertson – and the local crazies from the Ohio River valley who flooded the local radio airways with variously 'old-time', or 'feel-good', or 'prosperity' gospels and perpetual appeals for 'seed offerings' and 'love gifts'.

Many late Saturday nights or early Sunday mornings, crawling into bed beside Clare, bits and pieces of his sermon still tumbling through his brain, Adrian would press himself to the warm bend of his wife's buttocks, and reaching beneath her night shirt, cup one of her breasts in his hand and bury his face in her long hair, which always smelled to him like Eden. Unfailingly that verse that held how *the word became flesh and dwelt among us'* would come to him, along with the prayer that she might wake sufficiently to allow him to dwell among her flesh entirely.

In their early years, before Damien and Sarah, before she returned to school, before he and his work and their dull routines in what she'd begun to call 'Finally', Ohio, had become the focus for her discontent, Clare would often give in to this ritual seduction, signaling by a tiny sigh, a catch of her breath, or a little moan, or by pushing her rump more firmly against him, or by rolling on her back and moving his hand with her hand between her legs while still seeming to be deep in sleep. Afterward, as she curled back into her private slumber, the wordless discourse of their lovemaking done, Adrian would count his blessings, giving thanks for the gift of his wife while replaying the tape of his freshly typed sermon in his mind, tapping out the phrases such as he could remember them, word by word, syllable by syllable, with his fingers tapping on Clare's beautiful bottom, a private code the cadence of which would put him eventually to sleep.

In the weeks since she had left him, his homiletics, even Dr. Hinkston, the senior pastor, commented, had become suddenly 'more moving, more engaged, more relevant somehow, more meaningful.'

'A gift of the Holy Spirit, the fiery tongue!' Dr. Hinkston called it, but Adrian figured it might be the drink that Francis Concannon and he had gotten in the habit of overdoing on Saturday nights, and the low-grade, ever-present, and flickering rage, the mysteries of human suffering and passion, the cross and flame his life had become.

FATHER FRANCIS Concannon couldn't care less about that. His anger was no mystery at all.

'For fuck's sake, Adrian,' the priest shouted over the phone, 'next time I get word about a friend in trouble from a horse's ass instead of the horse's mouth, I'm gonna really be pissed.'

'I'm sorry, Francis, I should have called.'

Word of his friend's trouble had got to him at St. Michael's as gossip from one of his church ladies.

'At least we don't have to worry about your missus running off with an artist, Father!' said Mrs. Bokuniewicz one Tuesday in late June after morning Mass.

The priest had been a true friend ever since, coming over to

Adrian's without invitation, bringing pizza and beer, chicken chop suey, a bag of burgers and fries, and a bottle of Irish, sitting up with Adrian those summer nights in the first weeks of his single parenthood. And when Adrian would take the kids up to bathe them and tuck them into bed and say their prayers, the priest would tidy up downstairs, picking up the toys, folding the laundry, cleaning up the kitchen, feeding the kitten and the dog. Then he'd fix two tumblers of what he called 'Dunphy's damage' – generous measures of bronze-colored liquor poured from a green bottle over ice cubes, and insist that Adrian sit out on the screened porch and tell him everything.

'That's the stuff, boyo,' the priest would say in a stage-Irish brogue, taking a long sip of the whiskey, 'St. Patrick's holy water itself. Any fucking wonder they call it "spirits"!'

Adrian would sip from his own glass, wince with the burn of it, exhale deeply, and settle into the chair with one ear tuned for the children upstairs, glad to have the priest sharing the watch with him. On such nights the general panic that he'd felt since Clare had left him would subside, if only for the couple of hours that the two men sat out on the screened porch, in the dark, watching the evening traffic on Lima Avenue go by and the streetlamps attracting bugs and the bats circling in the night air.

He'd been so frightened that something would happen to Damien or Sarah. It was an ever-present fear, a general dread, a constant wariness that something bad would happen to them if he let down his guard. He'd always had it, but it was doubled now that his wife had left him and he realized only half the eyes were keeping watch, half the ears were tuned toward their protection, only one body to place between them and peril. He was not sleeping very well. He was always tired. The giant frame of Francis Concannon, his thick hair wild on his head, his great jaw silhouetted by the yellow glow of the streetlamp, sitting on the other side of the small table on the screened porch was a comfort – as if, at least on such evenings, there was another protector in the house and Adrian's vigilance could be dialed down. In his Ohio State sweatshirt, a pipe smoldering in one hand, a glass of whiskey in the other, the priest made an unlikely sentry. But for Adrian his friendship had been a gift. All the area's Protestant clergy had sent polite epistles, promised prayers, cited Scriptures, encouraged him to get in touch if they 'could help in any way', but otherwise had kept their distance, as if spousal distemper and divorce were contagions and Adrian the local carrier. Father Concannon had broken the quarantine and entered the pesthouse. He had been unambiguously the friend in need. And Adrian was ever grateful. That he had become Adrian's de facto confessor had been another gift. The deepest secrets of his ruined heart had been dumped on the priest, his black anger and dark rages, his vengeful impulses toward Clare and her new lover – 'the motherfucker', Adrian seethed, because she was a mother and she left her children and 'he'll never love her like I loved her, he's only fucking her.' Sometimes he wept and the priest would reach across the table, take hold of Adrian's shoulder in his massive hand, and steady him till the worst was over.

'*Lacrimae* fucking *rerum*, pal,' he'd commiserate, 'the fucking tears of things.'

Adrian couldn't confide much to his senior pastor, the Reverend Hinkston, or to the Northwest Plains district superintendent, the Reverend Carlton Paul Ritter, or to the West Ohio Conference bishop, Bishop Wesley A. Maghee.

Nor could he imagine really having a drink, really letting his tongue get loosened with any of them. While they were his connectional and episcopal up-line, he knew that the failure of his marriage presented some difficulties for them. The scandal of a minister's wife running off with another man, leaving children behind, was a cup they'd rather God had let pass. A committee had already been formed at the church to monitor Adrian's 'changed status' and report to the district superintendent, who would report to the bishop.

To his credit, the Reverend Hinkston had at least made an effort, however clumsy. He'd told Adrian he'd be happy to counsel him and Clare and let it be known that he'd saved many marriages over his 'nearly forty years of servant ministry'.

'Cleta and I have met with many a young couple in distress, and prayed with them and set them right – it's all there in the book, you know, that's the guide. Sometimes all it takes is someone with a little more experience, you know, to remind us of the times we were in love. Cleta and I have gotten through many a crisis, and still been married forty-three years. Even sexual dilemmas can be gotten through.'

Adrian could not bring himself to tell the Reverend Hinkston that he did not want Clare back. Her having sex with other men was not a 'sexual dilemma'. It was betrayal. Her lack of remorse, her willingness to leave her children were all, for him, signs of moral or mental disorder, perhaps forgivable, even, he prayed, forgettable, but ultimately – he knew this in his heart of hearts – irreparable. Their deal was done. She had breached the central contract of their marriage, broken their household, reneged on their intimate agreements. That damage was done and could not be undone. They would all have to live with it, for better or worse. Whether madness or passion or unfortunate choices, whether she was just spreading her own wings, realizing her full potential, or just reaching her sexual prime and hungry for a little unfamiliar sex, he neither knew nor any longer wanted to know. He could live with the broken-ness, the worry over his children's well-being, the fears he had for the future. He could live with all of that. But he could no longer live with her. Whether this was unchristian, unholy, sinful, or immoral, whether work of the devil or Will of God, he couldn't say. And didn't care; it was what it was.

What Francis Concannon seemed to offer, since he first called Adrian and came barging into the wreckage of his family, was moral immunity, spiritual oasis, a kind of ecclesiastical safe harbor neither too shallow for the hard truth nor too fathom-less to obscure the sadness of it. He never quoted the Letters of Paul or the Gospel of Matthew or the Acts of the Apostles to Adrian. Rather, he had brought him food and drink and poems. He brought him time and the moment's safety. He brought his brother cleric the gift of his presence and manifest willingness to bear his portion of the grief and rage and fear. And sitting out on the screened porch, listening to crickets and watching lightning bugs, sipping their 'damage', Adrian found himself somehow comforted by the priest's recitations, his tipsy party-pieces, his bits of Yeats:

> Others because you did not keep
> That deep-sworn vow have been friends of mine;
> Yet always when I look death in the face,
> When I clamber to the heights of sleep,
> Or when I grow excited with wine,
> Suddenly I meet your face.

or Beckett:

> *I would like my love to die*
> *and the rain to be raining on the graveyard*
> *and on me walking the streets*
> *mourning her who thought she loved me.*

Even an anonymous, possibly medieval bard who claimed:

> *The way to get on with a girl*
> *Is to drift like a man in the mist,*
> *Happy enough to be caught,*
> *Happy to be dismissed.*

> *Glad to be out of her way,*
> *Glad to rejoin her in bed,*
> *Equally grieved or gay*
> *To learn that she's living or dead.*

The lilt and faux brogue the priest achieved in the recitation of his poems unfailingly made Adrian laugh or weep. The drink assisted.

Best of all of them, Adrian thought, was Philip Larkin. 'That awful man', Francis Concannon called him, and gave out with line after line by heart:

> *There is regret. Always, there is regret.*
> *But it is better that our lives unloose,*
> *As two tall ships, wind-mastered, wet with light,*
> *Break from an estuary with their courses set,*
> *And waving part, and waving drop from sight.*

Adrian so wanted to get past it all. He knew it would kill him if he did not let it go. He wanted to be free of it. To be restored to some kind of wholeness, beyond regret, beyond fear, beyond it all – yes, *two tall ships, wind-mastered, wet with light* – he wouldn't begrudge Clare any happiness, once he had been restored to his; once he had his new course set he'd happily wish her a good riddance: *and waving part, and waving drop from sight.* In the meantime, though, the dark wound still festered. She had harmed him and harmed his household and he did not wish her well.

NIGHTS AFTER the priest left Adrian slept better, not least because of the bottle of whiskey they would feel duty-bound to empty before they'd say good night. The priest would slump into his Buick and drive off to St. Michael's rectory and Adrian would quench the lights in the manse, promising again to slow down the drinking, thanking God, as he climbed the stairs, for friends like Francis, for the safety of his children on whose slumber he would always peek, bending to kiss them and to hear them breathe.

In his own bedroom he would strip, piss, brush his teeth, and crawl onto the mattress on the floor. Clare had taken the brass bed frame, bought at the Salvation Army store soon after they'd married, when she left. And the large Persian rug that had covered the pine floorboards – it went off rolled up in David Eason's Toyota van, and the oak dresser he'd refinished for her for one of their anniversaries and the matching beveled-glass mirror he'd found for Christmas one year – all of it gone – the fixtures and furnishings of their married life. He lay in the sheets ogling the breasts of the willing, come-hithering beauties in the pages of a girlie magazine he'd taken from an embarrassed teen at church when it fell from her school bag inadvertently. He would study their ankles and the curl of their feet, their tattoos and perfectly tonsured genitalia. He would try to imagine his hand on their breasts, then his mouth, then his ear placed over their sternum where he'd hear their heart beating life and longing. After masturbating, he'd pray to be spared the fate of Onan, who had spilled his seed in the Book of Genesis. He'd resolve to quit the drink, to be a better father, to accept his circumstances, and to do God's will and God's work in accordance with his calling. Whether it was drink or fatigue that made him sleep, he was glad for it whenever it came. If he dreamed, he did not remember it.

A NIGHT OF excess and a resolve to quit drinking had kept him abstemious for a couple of weeks. But the priest's phone call had left him little wiggle room for an excuse. Adrian did not want to go out that night. He'd not left the kids with a sitter since Clare had left. He had to prepare a sermon for the morning. Things were getting shaky at the church. Still, he knew he never could refuse the priest, and so resigned himself to be ready at five. He showered and shaved and put on a fresh pair of khakis, his brown penny loafers, a blue button-down shirt, and his dark blue sport coat.

WHETHER IT was the bag of books and crayons and paper, the fact that she was nearer their own size, or that she was the first adult female to stand at the kitchen table since their mother had left three months before, that drew his kids to

Mary De Dona, Adrian Littlefield had no idea. Either way, halfway through his list of child care guidelines – what they should eat, when they should go to bed, their family doctor's emergency numbers, his beeper number, the numbers for the police and fire and ambulance – Sarah was seated with her thumb in her mouth, picking crayons from the cigar box and drawing stick figures on a blank page that Mary De Dona had given her. Damien was explaining the decals on his skateboard to Mary De Dona, who sat listening intently to the boy.

'C'mon, Reverend Littlefield,' Francis Concannon pleaded, holding the back screen door open, 'the car's running, can't you see they'll be fine.'

'But I don't know anything about her', Adrian protested as the priest's car backed out of the driveway and made its way up Cory Street, past East Sandusky Street, to West Main Cross.

'For fuck's sake, Adrian, what's to know? She teaches fourth grade at our parish school. She's a woman. She's Italian. She knows more about kids than either of us will ever know. They'll be fine. We're taking the night off. We're on a mission.'

Still, when the priest stopped for gas before getting on the freeway, Adrian went into the station and called home to see if everything was all right.

'They're fine', Mary De Dona assured him. 'We're having grilled cheese sandwiches and then we're walking to Riverbend Park to feed the carp and do some people-watching.'

By the time they'd passed Toledo and crossed from Ohio into Michigan, Adrian knew there'd be no turning back.

'Where are we going, Francis?'

'Tijuana . . . relax. We'll be there before you know it.'

Just north of Monroe, the priest rolled up his car window,

lit up his pipe, and the car filled with the acrid smell of marijuana.

'I'm your designated driver tonight, Adrian, no boozola for me. Wanna toke?'

Adrian declined the pipe, but it hardly mattered. The car filled with a cloud of smoke and he could feel the sudden light-headedness he hadn't felt since his pre-seminary days at Wesleyan. The same idiot grin, the same stupid nodding as if he could agree with anything; the same hollow in his stomach – the priest was looking over and smiling inexplicably. Outside of Detroit, they opened the windows again and from under the driver's seat the priest pulled a bottle of aftershave and splashed the car and Adrian.

Crossing over the Detroit River on the Ambassador Bridge, Adrian was counting boats in the water below them when he was seized by a sudden panic. He was going into a foreign country in the company of an apparently crazy priest. He was a single parent from Findlay, Ohio, who'd left his minor children, two hours south, in the custody of an unknown Italian woman who might sell them to the circus or run off with them, for all he knew, or testify against him in some future trial brought by his ex-wife for negligence.

'Where in God's name are we going, Francis?' Adrian pleaded with the priest.

'For dinner in Windsor – and then the ballet. Aren't you hungry? I am starving, man.'

Adrian *was* hungry, and though utterly helpless, he could not work up any anger at the priest or make sufficient protest.

The light of late September was fading from the evening sky and the cities on either side of the river were bathed in the most inextinguishable light, and he decided to give it all to God – his children's safety, his shaky situation at St. Mark's, the sermon he had not prepared, the hapless prospects for his future, his damaged household, his pummeled heart, his hunger, his desire, his unfathomable want, the sores and boils of rejection he felt – all of it he was giving to God, as Job had in that god-awful comfortless book which had only ever raised in Adrian reasonable doubts. It didn't matter. And as they passed through Canadian customs, assuring the border agent that they were U.S. citizens, here for the evening only, and only for pleasure, Adrian turned to his guide and guardian, his pilot and protector, the dry but pleasantly stoned parish priest, and quoted, 'Blessed be the name of the Lord.'

'Back at you, brother', the priest smiled widely. 'Amen!'

AT MARIO'S on Ouellette Street, the priest ordered steaks and baked potatoes and a bottle of Bardolino.

'I was six months at the University of Padua', he told Adrian. 'I love their wines – all from the hill country around Verona. Romeo and Juliet, Lago di Garda, the Dolomites . . . *sei la più bella del mondo* . . . Goddammit Adrian, where goes the time?'

All Adrian could do was nod and sigh.

After dinner, the men walked up Ouellette Street to a place on the corner called Studio 4. The priest held the door for Adrian, who eyed him narrowly.

'Have no fear, Reverend Littlefield. Would I lead you astray?'

Inside it was dark and sparsely crowded. There were booths

and tables along the brick walls with candles on them. The middle space was one broad serpentine bar winding its way around through adjoining rooms with black-shirted bar men and women serving drinks on one side and on the other, men of all ages, some seated, some standing, all gazing upward at an odd parade of beautiful, awkwardly dancing girls, working their way at intervals along the bar in various stages of exotic undress, from partial to total nakedness.

'Oh God, Francis . . .' said Adrian. But he could not avert his eyes from their bodies, in general and in particular, and their smiles and their eyes which, the closer he got, seemed to bear him no apparent malice, rather seemed to understand how he was entirely enthralled, quite hopelessly fixed upon their beauty, quite beyond the province of reason or words. He had not seen a naked woman in months except in movies and magazines – the little stash of pornography he kept hidden in his bedroom closet. But these were live and moving beauties. He could smell their powders and perfumes. That he could not touch them was no bother. He only wanted to admire them and bless them for how they did not refuse his gaze.

It was late when they left Windsor, and Adrian was fairly drunk and the lights of the Detroit skyline shining off the river were, like everything, a blur to him. The U.S. Customs guard asked if they had anything to declare.

'Nothing' Father Concannon told him.

'Bringing any guns into Detroit?'

'No, nothing' the priest repeated.

'Maybe I should loan you one of mine!' the fat guard joked, and waved them on.

Adrian slept through Toledo and never woke when the

priest stopped for coffee in Bowling Green and had to be helped from the car at home.

'What a night, Francis', Adrian tried to say, as the priest helped him into the house and up the stairs, out of his clothes and into bed. Downstairs the priest found Mary De Dona curled on the couch in her own slumber, the TV flickering out some infomercial, the children's drawings on the coffee table. He shook her gently by the shoulder.

'I'm all right, Father, let it be.'

'Will I take you home?'

'Go on, Father, let it be.'

The priest stood straight and still, listening for the sounds of anything wrong in the house. No noise issued from upstairs where Adrian and his children were safely asleep. Only the hum of ceiling fans and appliances, the low and orderly breathing of Mary De Dona on the couch, and low din of the flickering TV – all was well, he reasoned, all was well.

Out on the porch Father Concannon pronounced a general absolution: '*Ego te absolvo a peccatis tuis in nomine Patris et Filii et Spiritus Sancti. Amen*', then drove home and slept the sleep of a child of God.

ADRIAN LITTLEFIELD dreamed he was whole again, his consortium restored, the body of a woman opening to him. In the dream she was a stranger to him, her habits a mystery, their desires new. The feel of her flesh under his fingers tingled with what were entirely new sensations; still, he knew that she knew that he knew that she knew. And her body was smaller than he might have remembered if he had remembered anything, which in his dream it was well known that he didn't. He had no past or future, only now. And her hair was darker and her sweet mouth lovelier and her parts in their own way accustomed to his. Oh God, Oh God, is all he could hear himself trying to say, because now that he thought of it God *is* love, and those who abide in love abide in God, and God . . . Oh Love, Oh Yes . . . Oh . . .

Wherever he was between awake and the dream, it was Mary De Dona astraddle him, pressing her little body onto his body, with one hand on his chest and with the other pressing her fingers to his open lips, whispering, 'Hush, Reverend Littlefield, let it be', still moving on him, though he had come already, still shoving herself against him, him holding her buttocks in his hands, pulling her forward and pressing her back, pressing his heels into the mattress, his head thrown back until she bent to kiss him on his mouth and on his head and then sitting back upright, because now he was hard again and turning her over and pressing himself deeper and deeper into her and her eyes closing and her mouth wide open and the room awash in new morning light and her two hands pulling him into her and she was finished and he was finished again and it was done. Adrian Littlefield rolled on his back, breathless and wide awake.

'Have you a cigarette?' she asked him.

'Cigarette? . . . Why, no . . .'

'*Porca miseria!* Are you good for anything?'

She was pulling her camisole over her head, and stepping into her panties, and buttoning her blue jeans and throwing the green sweatshirt over her with *St. Michael the Archangel* printed in gold and pulling her curly black hair back and knotting it in a bun. He had not noticed the night before how very comely she was – her rose skin, her brown eyes, the little figure of her standing right in front of him. He wondered at her age.

'Was your ex-wife beautiful?'

Adrian hadn't a clue what to say.

'I don't know . . . I suppose she was . . . I don't know . . . Why . . . ?'

'Your children are beautiful. I've got to go. They shouldn't see me here.'

'Wait' he called after her, but she was gone.

RUMMAGING THROUGH his sermon archives for something to say that Sunday morning, the Reverend Adrian Littlefield could not stop grinning. Nor could he focus on the titles of his collection: 'If It's Good It's God's' 'The Attitude is Gratitude' 'The Present's a Gift' 'The Corinthians Write Back.' He hustled Damien and Sarah into their Sunday clothes, brushed his teeth and gargled with mouthwash, put on his brown suit, and made for St. Mark's, wondering why he couldn't wipe the grin off his face. Nor could he make sense of the morning's readings – from Ezekiel and Psalms, Philippians and Matthew – all he could think of was the bend of her body, the taste of her shoulder, the smell of her hair, her inexplicable kindnesses. Had it been a dream? And rising to his homiletic duties, gazing into the faces of his people, he knew he had nothing to tell them. So he sang.

As for Father Francis Assisi Concannon, holding forth to the faithful at the ten o'clock Mass, he observed it was the Feast of Michael the Archangel and another Sunday in Ordinary Time.

V

I N THE Block Island phone book, Dr. Adrian Littlefield looked among the W's for Ben Walters. There was only one, on Pilot Hill Road. He pulled a map of the island from his back pocket. Pilot Hill Road ran a little ways southwest of town. He walked across the street to the taxi ranks near the boat docks and climbed in an old station wagon with *Island Hack & Taxi Tours* on it.

'Tour of the island?' the old woman at the wheel asked him.

'How long does it take?' he asked.

'How long do you have?'

'I have to be back for the four o'clock ferry.'

'No problem', she told him. 'That's acres of time. It really is a tiny island.'

Adrian got in and introduced himself.

'Adrian Littlefield' he extended his hand.

'Gloria, Gloria Dodge' she said. 'You're welcome to the island. First time here?'

'Yes, well . . . yes, my first time.'

She drove out of the parking lot and turned northward going out past the hotels, the local bars, the long beaches packed with sunbathers. Adrian kept a map and watched the sights and signposts go by. Gloria kept up the travelogue.

'The island is only seven miles long by three miles wide, shaped like a pork chop, less than eleven square miles.' Gloria had this 'tour' memorized. Adrian looked at his foldout map of the island which he'd been given by the tour organizers. Block Island did, indeed, look like a pork chop, with the narrow bony end to the north and the squat round meaty end to the south. There was a profusion of dune and seascape as they drove out of town.

'That's Scotch Beach there, a little rougher water. It was named for the people who didn't want to pay the dime a week to help with the upkeep of the beaches. They could swim there free.'

Adrian smiled and nodded and feigned interest. The old station wagon bumped along out what he read was Corn Neck Road past Bush Lot Hill toward Chaqum Pond at the north end of the island.

'Many people live here year-round?' he asked.

'I guess they figure around nine hundred now. Most of these homes are seasonals. People from Providence and Hartford and Boston and New York. Many of the same families come for generations. I've been here my entire life. We raised seven children here. Seventeen grandchildren and nine great-grandchildren. They'll all be coming home next week. My husband's birthday.'

'Wow' said Adrian, and looked out at the sea.

At the end of the road was a rock beach, a small parking lot, and off to the west an old lighthouse.

'1867 it was built. They're making it into a museum. My son is on the volunteer committee. If you want to get out and have a look, I'll wait. There's plenty of time.'

Adrian shook his head and she backed the car around to head back the road they'd come.

'How old will your husband be?'

'Well, he'd have been eighty but he died last year. Still, we figured we'd get together anyway, and celebrate, you know . . . it's all just family.'

'That must be very hard', said Adrian, a little worried that he'd gotten more information about Gloria than he ever wanted but figuring now there was no turning back.

'Well, of course, we all miss him terribly. He was the dearest man and the grandchildren were so sad, so beautiful . . . they wanted to have a cake and get out all the pictures. I can't wait to see them. They're coming from as far away as Denver. He was the dearest man, everybody's favorite. He always loved it when they came to visit us here on the island.'

'Won't that be nice', Adrian said. 'Look at those beautiful yachts!'

They'd come to the marina at the Great Salt Pond and the New Harbor area. Sailboats tied to their moorings rocked in the wide basin. Fashionably clad boaters walked up and down the docks. A restaurant called Dead Eye Dick's was doing a brisk luncheon trade. The old station wagon passed a small graveyard on the left.

'He's buried in there', said Gloria.

Adrian said nothing, hoping the conversation might take another turn.

'Fifty-eight years we were married. But we'd been 'together' for years before that. I met him when I was thirteen. It was February. I was ice-skating with friends and all they could do was laugh at me because I kept falling and I couldn't stand up. The legs would go right out from under me. They were all laughing. It was horrible. And all of a sudden, I look up and this boy is holding out a hockey stick to me. "Grab on," he says to me, "I'll pull you to shore." And after he had rescued me,

he sat me on a bench on the shore and knelt and untied my
skates and helped me on with my boots and I thought, What
a beautiful boy, what a beautiful boy.'

'You were very young', Adrian said. He was studying the
map as the road curved south, working its way down the west
side of the island. He plotted the winding route that would get
them eventually to Pilot Hill Road. Like it or not, Gloria was
giving him the full-course tour.

'Well, it was three years later. I was sixteen. I was walking
into town and he stopped his truck and asked if I wanted a lift.
And at first I said "No thanks" because I didn't want to be too
easy, but he just leaned over and said, "Are you sure?" and I
thought, Well... why not. I climbed in and we've been together
ever since. The day they bombed Pearl Harbor he asked me to
marry him. He knelt down just the way he had when he rescued
me that time, you know, to untie my skates, only this time he
asked me to marry him. And I thought what a beautiful man
he is. We had the wedding on New Year's Eve. It was 1941. He
left for the Navy three days later. He was a UDT man. Well,
you know, growing up on the island, he knew how to swim. I
was nineteen. He was twenty.'

Adrian looked at the old woman beside him and tried to
imagine her at nineteen. He tried to imagine what it took to
marry a man and sleep with a man who was leaving for war
and might never return. He wondered if she had been faithful to him. He wondered if he had been faithful to her. He
wondered if they discussed such things in those days.

'What was his name?' Adrian asked her.

'Bob. Well, Robert. Well, Bob . . . Bob Dodge.' Her eyes
were red and watering now. Saying his name aloud must have
triggered the tears. There was no sadness in her voice. Only

resignation. But her eyes were brimming with real tears. She was looking for something to wipe them with.

'I'm sorry, I don't know . . .'

'Oh no, no worry' Adrian said.

They'd nearly made it to the southeast corner of the island.

Gloria pulled into a parking area below another light-house.

'Take a walk out there and you'll be able to see the end of Long Island' she said, 'and Mohegan Bluffs and the Southeast Lighthouse. They had to move the thing back a few years ago. It would have fallen into the sea. And you can say you stood in Rhode Island and saw New York.'

Adrian had no interest in the lighthouse or Long Island or a walk in the sand but he figured Gloria might want a moment to recompose herself. So he got out and took the path out among the scrub trees and *Rosa rugosa* shrubs, to where a wooden deck overlooked the high bluffs and the beach maybe two hundred feet below. It was a breathtaking view and he opened his arms wide and closed his eyes and tilted his head back so his face basked fully in the brackish air and the bright sunlight and the slight breeze and the beauty of it. He stood and looked at the seascape. He looked back the way he'd come but everything had disappeared behind the dunes he'd walked through. He wondered how long it might take for Gloria to get herself together.

Below on the long beach he could see fishermen casting lines into the sea and reeling in and casting out again and further up the beach were figures of men and women – maybe a dozen or two dozen – outstretched on the strand taking the sun, and others running into the waves and back or diving into the pounding surf. The noise of the ocean and their voices seemed even more distant than he'd gauged at this height.

Out on the sea he could make out pleasure boats in their various odysseys, seabirds diving, what looked like schools of fish feeding on the surface. He wondered how long he'd have to watch and if the season was the right one to see a whale or a dolphin, or great sea turtles coming ashore to lay their eggs, or any of the countless other creatures that would never appear in Findlay, Ohio, no matter how long one looked out into the light or dark. There were cloud banks in the distance and the line between the sea and the sky, and what he reckoned might be the edge of Long Island far in the distance, grew less and less articulate and for a moment he wondered if he might be entirely lost.

VI

THE MEETING with the bishop had gone fairly badly. In retrospect, Adrian was not surprised. This was Ohio and these were the 1980s, and they were Methodists and what did he expect the bishop to do?

'It's not', Bishop Maghee was eager to assure him, 'that Clare left you, or the divorce, or that your children might be scandalized', though he felt duty-bound to cite, in the prayer he began the audience with, that caution from the Gospel Matthew, to wit: *If any of you put a stumbling block before one of these little ones who believe in me, it would be better for you if a great millstone were fastened around your neck and you were drowned in the sea . . . Woe to the one by whom the stumbling block comes.*

Nor was it the 'very reasonable' concern about a suddenly single man with, 'let us say, adult desires', ministering to churchwomen made vulnerable by their 'religious dilemmas'. 'Clerical continence' was not the issue. Though the bishop was pained to remind him, it was not unheard of – a clergyman preying on a parishioner or vice versa.

'Romance and religious fervor are so often confused.'

It was simply the concern the bishop had for Reverend Littlefield's emotional well-being which seemed, if reports were even partially true, something he ought to be tending to. And all he was recommending, after all, all he was actually insisting upon, all he had actually conferred with the district superintendent and Reverend Hinkston about was a 'little respite' from pastoral duties – neither millstone nor drowning – only a temporary 'leave of absence' until after the holidays; three months of personal reflection, 'with pay of course', during which time both Adrian and the good people at St. Mark's could 'reassess their relationship.'

The bishop gave Adrian a list of 'Christian counselors', approved by the district, none with offices nearer to Findlay than Toledo and Cleveland, who would be 'helpful and discreet' and who would bill the UMC directly for 'up to six months of therapy and an evaluation'.

'We must take care of the caretakers, Adrian, minister to the minister – that's what we are called to do!' said Bishop Maghee, and looking at his wristwatch, extended a hand for Adrian to shake.

❖   ❖   ❖

'FOR FUCK'S sake, Adrian, what'd you say?' Father Francis Concannon was no stranger to the ways of bishops.

He and Adrian were sitting in the leather wingback chairs in the library at St. Michael's Rectory the day after the Reverend Littlefield had been called to see the bishop of the Western Ohio Conference of the United Methodist Church.

'What could I say? "He who sings prays twice"?'

'Of course you're right. It's like farting at skunks – trying to gainsay a bishop. The whores.' Father Concannon said 'whores' to rhyme with 'lures', and added, 'The fucking wankers . . . my own's a dodgy client just like yours.'

The priest had made tea and was pouring it.

'I gave him all the ammo he'd need, what with the singing. And of all things, Beatles tunes.'

'The Pentecostals would call it talking in tongues. And brought the snakes in for you to fucking dazzle.'

THE REVEREND Adrian Littlefield, recently quit by his adulteress wife, recently angry and lonely and bone tired of the duties of single parenting, recently despairing, recently at wit's end over his prospects, recently drunk, recently stoned, recently a patron of a topless-bottomless bar in Windsor, and only a matter of hours after having sex with his children's babysitter, whose first name he could remember but whose surname had escaped him, had stood in the sanctuary under the massive stained-glass likeness of Christ his Lord and before the faithful congregants of St. Mark's United Methodist Church on South Main Street in Findlay, Ohio, and, uncharacteristically lost for words, cleared his throat, opened his arms as Moses before the Red Sea, and raising his inexplicably grinning face heavenward, instead of commencing a sermon, sang out, off-key but enthusiastically, in evident praise and thanksgiving for all of his recent iniquities:

> *When I find myself in times of trouble*
> *Mother Mary comes to me*
> *Speaking words of wisdom, let it be.*
> *And in my hour of darkness*
> *She is standing right in front of me*
> *Speaking words of wisdom, let it be.*
> *Let it be, let it be.*

He stepped from behind the oaken pulpit, stationed himself in front of the altar, and smiling widely, raised his voice again.

> *And when the broken hearted people*
> *Living in the world agree*
> *There will be an answer, let it be.*
> *For though they may be parted there is*
> *Still a chance that they will see.*
> *There will be an answer, let it be.*

He was into the next verse though he wasn't entirely sure he knew it, *And when the night is cloudy, there is still a light that shines on me . . .* and might have even made some sense of all of it, but the Reverend Dr. Hinkston, his senior pastor, sensing something in his associate's manner was terribly amiss, and worried that the eleven o'clock service was about to go seriously off-track, rose from his seat behind the pulpit and led the people in polite applause, then wordlessly, by nod and glaring, signaled the ushers at the back of church to pass the plates for the offering. A couple of spiky-haired teens dressed in black and emblazoned with tattoos and seated with their perpetually embarrassed parents, arose during Adrian's brief solo and, thrusting their fists into the air, took up the chorus: *Let it be, let it be, let it be, let it be, whisper words of wisdom, let it be,* while one air-keyboarded the piano chords and the other air-guitared the heavy bass notes of the refrain, all the while nodding their spiky heads furiously in time. Marilyn Rubritus, the unmarried and, it was rumored, heavily medicated daughter of the long-widowed Geraldine Rubritus, stood in the middle of the pew she and her mother had occupied quietly for nearly half a century, unknotted her long silver hair from the bun it had been in all her life, till it fell in quick luxuriant waves over the red cashmere sweater she always wore to church, and began to sway with the singing rhythmically, her arms outreaching and her palms upturned, her bony shoulders and skinny hips achieving a kind of tidal sway, and the look on her face one of ecstasy, the way you'd imagine young hippie girls at Woodstock years before. Cleta Locey, the organist, never one to be caught off guard, had taken up the tune, which of course she knew, while the Reverend Hinkston tried, from his side of the sanctuary, to eyeball her to quit and the ushers moved with the gilded plates up the aisles and everyone, reaching for their tithes and offerings, looked back and forth at one another wondering what it was they had just witnessed. It had lasted only a couple of minutes, but it was sufficiently outside the pale of their erstwhile church experiences that they knew something unforeseen and unplanned had happened.

'Did you see them,' whispered Adrian, still grinning like a simpleton, 'the heavenly hosts?' as Reverend Hinkston led him to the vestry, while the bell choir, after a series of dagger looks from the senior pastor, and accustomed to playing for time, took up their rendition of 'How Great Thou Art'.

After removing his stole and cincture and robe, and following the Reverend Hinkston's directive, Adrian collected his children from their Sunday school classes, loaded them in the family Honda, and drove them home. He sang all the way home. And because he could not keep from grinning, Damien and Sarah grinned back at him. For the first time in months they all looked joyous.

'I TELL YOU, Francis, it was the closest thing to inspiration I have ever felt – the breath of God – as if I'd been suddenly loosed from the bonds of gravity and routine. Always before, I'd be trying to say something that'd touch their souls while they'd all be trying not to fall asleep. But this was different. I tell you, Francis, I felt *alive* and they looked *alive* to me. For the first time I looked out over that little sea of faces and saw them all as fellow pilgrims. Not fellow United Methodists, or fellow Christians, or fellow sinners. Just fellow humans in search of the way home. And I could see that what they didn't need was another sermon. It's as if I could see myself in them: hapless and lonely, holy and free, all of us somehow in it together, Francis, just trying to find our way, wondering if we're ever going to make it.'

The priest nodded and smiled and sipped his tea while Adrian carried on.

'It was an apparition. They looked like innocents, Francis. Angels – every one of them. I tell you, I could see their wings. I could see them readying to take flight, Cora Perkins, fat Bill Wappner, the grievous Fielding couple with their punk-rock twins. They just all looked so lovely to me – these people whose people I've been burying and marrying and baptizing. Poor Marilyn Rubritus, old Henry Richardson in his wing-tips and banker's suit, Art Geyer with his homely wife, the Morris sisters, just turned fourteen and fifteen, proud of their new figures, the way boys are suddenly watching them; Freda Chambers with her goiter and bug eyes, they all looked like cherubim and seraphim and archangels. And all I wanted was to tell them that everything was going to be all right. Everything would turn out fine – I could see it all, Francis – they'd all be just fine and flying again.'

'A beatific vision!' Father Francis said. 'Was that some dope or what!'

'It wasn't the dope, Francis', Adrian said. 'I think it started after Mary . . . what's her name?'

The priest sat up in the wingback, set his mug on the side table, and leaned into the conversation.

'Mary De Dona? What about her?'

'Well, she came to me in the night. There was this dream and I just woke up and she was . . . *there.*'

'*There?*'

'Well, she was on top of me, and she was naked, and, well . . .'

'The beatific vision!' Father Concannon sat back, pressed his head into the high back of the chair, smiling broadly.

Adrian looked puzzled.

'A "pastoral" visit!' The priest was evidently not surprised. 'God bless her. Now there's a woman with really priestly instincts.'

◆   ◆   ◆

FATHER FRANCIS Assisi Concannon explained to the Reverend Adrian Littlefield how, ever since she'd come to St. Michael the Archangel's parish school, Mary De Dona had made known to him the depth of her devotions. She had expressed in a variety of ways her willingness to do whatever she could to assist him in his priestly mission. She had arrived in Findlay the year before to replace one of their retiring teachers. Little was known about her. She had answered their ad in the *Ohio Catholic*. She had her teaching certificate and was Catholic, or Italian at least, and parochial schools couldn't be that particular since they paid a good deal less than the public schools. And she was wonderful with the children. That much was obvious from the start. They all loved her and all of the parents loved her and the other teachers all approved as well. Even the nun who served as principal of the school and was famously cranky and stingy with praise, spoke glowingly about Mary De Dona.

'We rented her one of the condos we'd made, in the former convent, off the parking lot. Just behind here. Can't get nuns to live in them anymore. Well, can't get nuns anymore, period. But Mary was delighted with the space, the stained-glass windows and tiny rooms, the smell of Murphy's Oil Soap on the woodwork. She moved in with her dog and easels and books and that was that.'

The priest recounted to Adrian how one night the winter previous, she had come to the rectory greatly agitated, with her huge black dog in tow and begging for a blessing on the beast.

'It was late and I was alone here, sitting up watching *Hill Street Blues*, and she said the dog wasn't well, couldn't sleep, and would I bless it. Of course I thought she's some kind of a headcase, out there in her bathrobe with red boots on and a stocking cap and the wind lashing and the snow piled everywhere. But I wanted to get back to the TV so I blessed the thing, a quickie, but blessed it nonetheless, and said I hoped that would do it, but she insisted I use some holy water. So before I know it, I've got the two of them – this huge dog and this tiny woman in her nightdress, standing in the vestibule of the rectory, dripping with the weather, and I'm off looking for holy water, with which I eventually drench the two of them – Dante, the dog, that's what she calls it, and Mary De Dona – and bless them both in Latin for fuck's sake and she's shivering with the cold and I'm holding open the door for them, and she reaches up behind my head, stands on her tiptoes, and kisses me. On my own mouth! Then off she goes with goddamn Dante, shouting "Thank you Father, thank you Father" all over the neighborhood.'

'I never knew you anointed dogs', said Adrian.

'Well, we usually don't, except on the feast of my own name-sake. It's coming up next week, in point of fact. We do cats and canaries, dogs and goldfish. We'll bless, as the fellow said, "all creatures great and small". But she was in a panic, what could I do? And she told me it was a "Catholic" dog. Couldn't I see that by the white cross on its chest and its obvious piety – a fucking headcase – still, harmless enough, is what I thought.'

'The next night she came over about the same time. She had a plate of brownies. She looked, well, done up, you know. She had some perfume on. She said that Dante had crawled into bed beside her and slept like a baby and she was forever in my debt and would do anything at all to repay the kindness. "Anything, Father", she kept saying with those eyes of hers looking up at me, "anywhere, anytime, anything at all, Father." I thought she was going to break into that James Taylor tune.

I won't say she made a pass at me, Adrian, but there is about Mary De Dona a generosity of spirit I've not encountered in our species before.'

'Did you have sex with her, Francis?'

'No, no I didn't . . . really . . . couldn't.'

'You're a better man than I am then.'

'Not better, Adrian, just different.'

That his friend could be so tolerant of sin in general and yet so scrupulous in the observance of his priestly vows was at once both perplexing and impressive.

'So what did you tell her about me, Francis? That I was abandoned and desperate and horny?'

'I told her you needed a babysitter. I said that we needed a night out. And yes, I think I mentioned that you were on your own . . . and might have said something about loneliness. I'm not sure I ever used the word *divorce*. Nor did I say that Clare had left you, I'm sure I didn't. Only that you were a good man, dealt a bad hand, and we needed a night off.'

'Well, I'll have plenty of time off now, it seems.'

'The blighters,' Father Concannon seethed, 'the fucking wankers.'

THE FLOWERS that Adrian Littlefield took to call on Mary De Dona were sunflowers. The vase that she put them in was fluted and blue. She stood at the kitchen sink, in her condo in the former convent, cutting the ends of stems, setting them into the vase, waiting for Adrian to think of something to say.

'You shouldn't have. They're beautiful.'

The black dog that had barked fiercely when Adrian walked up the porch steps and sniffed his groin and buttocks when he entered the house now lay on the floor at the woman's feet eyeing Adrian warily.

'I wanted to say how very grateful I was –'

'Grateful?'

'For the other night.'

He wanted to tell her it had been like grace to him, the way she'd given herself, the way she'd come to him. It was free, abundant, unearned, a gift. Amazing grace, he wanted to say. He wanted to tell her that she had saved his life and restored to him a sense of worthiness. He wanted her to know how damaged he had felt, after Clare had left him, after his marriage failed, how he'd been despairing and depressed and beside himself and how ever since the other night he'd been filled with an inextinguishable sense of general benignity, and that even though he'd been suspended by his bishop from all pastoral duties and hadn't a clue what he was going to do next, he was certain he'd been changed for the better and immeasurably improved by what had happened between them the other night. He had rehearsed words to this effect but could not think of how to say them.

'I'm grateful too', she said. 'It was lovely. Do you want to do it again?'

'What?'

'Do you want to have sex with me again?'

There was such decorum about her speech, a daintiness, at odds, it occurred to Adrian, with the boldness of her question.

'Well, yes, but . . . Yes, of course I do.'

'Who's watching your children?'

'Francis . . . well, Father Concannon. He's taking them for burgers and a movie – *The NeverEnding Story*.'

'How very good of him.'

Mary De Dona set the sunflowers in the blue vase on the kitchen table, banished her giant dog to the back porch and the fenced yard, and took Adrian's hand and led him upstairs to the tiny room that was her bedchamber. She closed the door behind them, lit a small candle on the bedside table, pulled the curtains by, and turned to face him. Then she slowly, wordlessly, removed his clothing and just as slowly, wordlessly, removed her own. Whereupon the two of them fell into intimate if predictable embraces, kissing and licking, touching and sucking, holding and beholding and savoring each other for all of an hour, then another. Then they bathed together in her tub. She dried his back and rubbed some scented oil on him, and let his hands rub some of it on her, and though they agreed he really should be going, that surely *The NeverEnding Story* would be over now, before he could bring himself to put his clothes back on, he fell to his knees and pressed his face against her, whereupon they took up their embracing in earnest again.

Stretched out on Mary De Dona's narrow bed watching the ceiling fan slowly circling above them, Adrian could not keep from thinking about the latter days of Job, blessed by the Lord with fourteen thousand sheep, six thousand camels, a thousand yoke of oxen, and a thousand donkeys. He thought he might see his children and his children's children and die old and full of days.

'SEX WITH a generous stranger', wrote the Reverend Adrian Littlefield, in the first paragraph of what would become *Good Riddance*, 'is balm to the wounds of the broken-hearted.' He searched that sentence for something wrong, at odds as it seemed with his religious training, but in his own ears it rang entirely true.

The visitations of Mary De Dona had been a balm to him.

'Divorce is not, it turns out, the worst that can happen. The sky does not fall. The clocks do not stop. The buses run on schedule. Life goes on. The world is full of possibilities.'

It was consorting with Mary De Dona – the illicit sound of which exited him – that made him certain of these things and emboldened him to write them down. Their copulations – from the Latin for 'fastened together' – had restored his faith in divine providence. Fastened together with Mary De Dona was, he was certain, a state of grace. It always left him grinning and grateful, dreaming in all tenses and feeling infused with what he took to be gifts of a holy spirit. If he did not speak in tongues, the two of them no less spoke with tongues and fingers and mouths and hands, with the caught breath and perfect hush of touching, and all of the interlocking, interweaving, intersecting limbs and parts that had become the parties to their intercourse, such as it was. They hardly spoke. What more was there to say?

She came over on Tuesdays and Thursdays in the evening. She'd play with Sarah and Damien, help with their dinner and bedtimes, sometimes throw in a couple of loads of laundry and tidy the house, then make love to Adrian Littlefield, like any other household duty or routine chore. This too excited him, her matter-of-factness with him. Then she'd go home. On Saturdays, he'd arrange a babysitter, and go to the former convent where she lived, bringing fresh flowers and massage oil, eager to repay her lovely body for all the kindnesses it had shown his during the week.

'I want to worship at the altar of your every pleasure', he would whisper.

'Hush, churchman! On your knees! Come into the holy of holies', she replied, with a come-hither smile, feigning sacrilege and shyness, taking him by the hand to her tiny room. 'Light the candles, like a good altar boy.'

'GOD IS good', he wrote with newfound conviction, 'and has given us each other to magnify that goodness.'

'Paul was wrong', he wrote in a line that would later be quoted in and out of context. 'It is good for a man to touch a woman, and good for a woman to touch a man.'

Paul's confusion of sex and sin seemed to Adrian at odds with the essence of human nature. How, he asked himself, could the goodwill he bore toward Mary De Dona, the gift he saw her as, the grace he felt awash in when with her, the thanks that was overflowing in him since she came to him, the sign he reckoned that she was of God's love – how could it all be anything but good? What sin could leave one so manifestly at one with creation, at peace with one's being and another's? In Mary De Dona all the dull notions he'd studied in seminary were happily incarnate – resurrection, reconciliation, communion, and rebirth. She was Easter, Christmas, epiphany and apocalypse, a blessing and beatitude, a feast for his soul. Christ might have gone to the cross for him, but Mary De Dona had come to bed with him. Jesus might have raised himself from the dead, but Mary De Dona had restored Adrian to life itself – the life of the body and the mind and spirit that had been killed by the failure of his marriage. Paul was wrong. Adrian knew it now. And if Paul could be wrong, why not James and

John and Job and the rest? Not entirely wrong, just occasionally. Just enough for reasonable doubt, a little wiggle room for
questioning – that was all he was trying to establish. What if
the Bible was only a book, the authors of it merely men who
felt, for reasons he could now more fully comprehend, inspired
by the loving breath of God?

How had it taken him so long to arrive at this intelligence?
It made him want to read it more closely. It made him love the
words and fear them less. As human text, a record of mortals
searching for glimpses of God, it was engaging and inspiring.
As holy writ, inerrant transmissions through prophets and
apostles, it seemed as silly now as all pronouncements of infal-
libility. Still, Adrian had to admit to himself that until very
recently, he had accepted the King James Bible as God's Word
dictated to and carefully transcribed by such scriveners as God
has chosen for reasons best known to God and God alone.

And it was Paul, that great poser and epistler, that first circuit rider in the cause of Christ, the model for John Wesley's
bold remark that 'the world is my parish', whom Adrian now
read with the grain of salt that put the wonder into everything,
everything. For never was a man more wrong about women,
and therefore wrong about the men who coupled with them,
than Paul was when he wrote to the Corinthians. That Paul
regarded men as brutes and women as temptresses, fit only to
keep each other from 'incontinency', and marriage as a better
station than passionate, erotic sex, but not as good as celibacy,
struck Adrian as unfair to women like Mary De Dona, who
seemed to him quite proper vessels and dispensers of God's
mercy and grace. To be welcomed into another's bed, into
another body, not for the promises you might make, or the

shelter you might provide, or the babies you might bear or sire or for all the future possibilities, but rather for the gifts you might bring to the here and now, the moment at hand, not the past or future or pluperfect tense, but for the moment at hand – now there's the thing, thought Adrian, the gift like grace.

God is love, he quoted the beloved apostle, *and he who abides in love abides in God and God in him*. Whenever Adrian replaced the word *love* in this dictum with the name of Mary De Dona, apart from the idolatry, the sentence rang entirely true. He felt reborn, re-created, and alive in her.

By Halloween he had over a hundred pages. Part rant, part methodical reasoning – it had become his manifesto, a statement of faith in flux.

'We are God's gifts to one another. We come to one another like grace – out of the blue.'

By Thanksgiving he sent what turned out to be the first three chapters to an agent in New York who sent back an agreement for Adrian to sign which gave 15 per cent of any sale to the agency.

When a check came in the first week of January for over forty thousand dollars, he could not help but see in it the saving hand of God, coming as it did in the same mail as a letter from the district supervisor detailing how, 'after prayerful reflection and full consideration of the needs of the faithful in the Western Ohio Conference, we feel some changes have to be made.'

'The second half of the advance will be paid upon delivery of the completed manuscript', wrote Adrian's agent from New York. 'Get to work.'

'We'd like to offer you a chance to truly expand your ministry through our Pastoral Exchange Program', wrote the district supervisor. There was a pamphlet on the Worldwide Ministerial Exchange of the United Methodist Church and a 'call' to trade places for three months with 'the Reverend Gilson Miller and his family' from somewhere unpronounceable in England.

'The "geographic cure",' said Francis Concannon. 'Bishops are mad for it. Outta sight, outta mind. First they move ya, then they lose ya!'

'Might be good for the children, a change of venue, a chance to see a bit of the world.' Mary De Dona said travel was good education. 'Three months will go by in a blink.'

'Would you come with us?' Adrian asked her.

'An international scandal?' she laughed.

She thanked him for asking but said it would be better for him to travel light. She had her work to do and he had his.

HE HAD never heard the voice of God or seen anything that made him certain of God's direction. His 'calling' to the ministry of the Methodist Church had never been a road to Damascus experience. It had happened to him like the rest of life had – the slow accumulation of events, some memorable or remarkable, most others not, which taken together had become his life.

Things happen as they are supposed to happen, Adrian told himself. If God did not speak to him, he thought, God was nonetheless the one in charge. This was largely a default position, faith arrived at by the servants' door. If Adrian was not in charge of all that happened – and he clearly wasn't – and yet unable to abide the prospect of no one in charge, then God was whoever was left in the room. This was the only article of faith he still clung to: there was a God and he was not it. So life happened the way it was supposed to happen. If God wasn't directing things, God was at the least watching. Everything might not work out for the best, but everything would be over soon. It was enough on most days to keep him going forward, this knowledge that whoever was in charge here was carrying on.

He put thirty thousand of his windfall down on the big vacant mansion down the street from the church on the better-than-even chance there'd be no job waiting at St. Mark's when he came back from England. At least, he figured, they'd have a home. He left ten thousand with Mary De Dona with instructions to 'do it up the way you'd like it', and in his heart of hearts imagined them maybe getting married or moving in together when he returned, absence making their hearts grow fonder, he hoped.

After clearing it with Clare's attorney, he got passports, took the kids out of school, and in the first week of March, Mary De Dona drove Adrian and Damien and Sarah to Detroit, where they boarded an overnight flight for London. Thence on a train to Leeds in west Yorkshire, changing trains to the village of Hebden Bridge, where one of the congregants from Heptonstall met them at the station and drove the jet-lagged pilgrims further up into the Pennines to the stone manse that would be their home until the first of June. Looking out over what he'd read was the Caldervale, across the valley to hill fields rising up from the river below, Adrian Littlefield gave thanks for safe journeys and prayed for his children's well-being and his own.

VII

'Great view, isn't it!'
       'Yes, yes it is, spectacular.'
Gloria was leaning on the station wagon, finishing a smoke, recomposed.

'Could you see Long Island?'

'I don't know. Things kept appearing, then disappearing. Hard to know where the sea gives way to the land or sky. Everything kept blurring into everything else. But yes, yes, beautiful.'

They got back into the car; Gloria started the engine and backed out the drive. Adrian looked at his map to figure the route back to New Shoreham and the Old Harbor. There were still two hours before the return ferry.

'Do you know Pilot Hill Road?' Adrian asked. 'Do you know someone by the name of Ben Walters?'

'There was a Walters up that way all right. Just above Tug Hole. His wife was sick in some way. I think she died. Summer people from New York. He painted. You know, pictures. I don't know if he still comes or not. Do you want to go by there? How do you know them?'

'Friend of the family', Adrian said. 'If you've got the time, I'd like to have a look.'

He didn't know exactly what he wanted to find. He'd never really sorted out his thoughts on the matter. He didn't know what he was supposed to feel or think about it. Ben Walters had only been the first of the infidelities he was sure of. There might have been others before him. It hardly mattered now. He remembered a time when he hated the name and the idea of another man touching his wife in that way. He'd tried to outgrow those primitive feelings. He could remember, as a much younger man, wishing for the kind of marriage Gloria had had – those long years, those children and grandchildren and great-grandchildren, that love and grief and routine. Adrian could remember the times as a young family man driving through small towns in Ohio with Clare on a Sunday afternoon, looking into the tall windows of turn-of-the-century homes with their gingerbread and clapboard and backyard gardens, trying to imagine the orderly good-old-days lives of the inhabitants of such places, where everyone had a huge front porch on which they sat in the evening drinking lemonade and telling stories and waving at the neighbors who'd be walking by. He could remember how he awoke one morning to find he had the very thing, a settled life in Findlay, Ohio, in an old house with a wide porch and wooden floors and knickknacks and radiators and a wife whose unhappiness seemed to grow in direct proportion to his happiness. He'd wanted that life, the settled, Sunday dinner with the family, Rockwell print of an existence where he'd eventually be the senior pastor of a thriving church where everyone knew everyone and everyone's business and kept an eye out for each other's children and were determined to live happily ever after.

At about the same time Clare was getting tired of all of that. She wanted to know if he'd consider moving to New York. He could maybe manage one of her Uncle Harold's companies. They could live in Westchester. There would be more money, she was sure. He could commute to the city by train like Uncle

Harold did, to his office in midtown. She could do photography or videos or something artistic and the kids could get a nanny or go to a fashionable day care center and then to a Montessori school. She could come into the city on Friday nights for the theater; they could ice-skate at the rink at Rockefeller Center as she had done as a girl visiting Uncle Harold after her mother and father divorced. They would have interesting friends, an interesting life. She was tired of Ohio and Findlay and the First Methodist Church. She didn't want to be a senior pastor's wife. She didn't want a summer place on Lake Erie. She didn't want to grow old in an old house in the Midwest with a man who was content to be going nowhere.

He told her he thought there were no geographic cures. 'Unhappiness', he told her, in the way she hated that ministers had of speaking in slogans, 'was portable. Discontent travels light.'

Gloria had turned up High Street and it turned to a dirt road at Pilot Hill and she broke suddenly at the entrance to a small two-track drive on the right.

'I think that's the Walters place up there. Go ahead, I'll wait. Take your time.'

Adrian hadn't a clue what he was supposed to do, or what it was he wanted to find. What if Ben Walters was there and knew who he was? Maybe he'd read one of his books, or seen him on *Oprah* or heard him on the radio and knew the connections. What if he didn't know Adrian's connections to the woman he had seduced here almost twenty years ago and how it changed all their lives and left his children motherless and him with his hands full of duty and detail? What if he was only a withered old man walking around in tennis shorts and

sandals with leathery skin and a bald head? What would they
have to say to each other?

Adrian could feel his heart racing as he worked his way up
the little gravel drive to the clearing in the woods where a little
cedar-shingled cottage appeared surrounded by a little lawn
with a few old Adirondack chairs in a semicircle and badly
in need of paint. The place was tiny, a story and a half with a
screened porch, inside of which was what looked like the main
door. There was no sign of life anywhere around. No car, no
open windows, the grass a little overgrown. He tried the screen
door, walked in, and knocked at the main door and listened
hard for the sound of any movement inside. There was none.
He tried the doorknob but it was locked.

There was nothing. Only the sound of catbirds in the thick
woods around the place, and the smell of the sea, and the movement of the breeze in the greeny things around the place. There
was as well the small noise of a wind chime hanging from a
hawthorn tree in the yard, and at a distance, as he listened,
the noise of children down the hill near what he guessed was
the fresh water pond he'd seen on the map at the base of the
hill. Adrian looked in the window. The interior was small and
dark. A table at one end of the kitchen. A fieldstone fireplace
at one end of the main room, and a small hallway leading to
what must be the bedroom, or bedrooms – maybe two. There
were no signs of recent life inside the house.

Adrian walked around to the bedroom window. Through
the sheer curtains he could see an old metal bed, a bureau, and
a chair. Off to one side were a sink and a mirror. The bed was
made. There was no disorder to the room.

He looked out across the yard. There was a small shed with

windows and a small porch. It was, he reckoned, the artist's studio. He looked inside and saw an easel and a table and jars full of brushes and rags hung from hooks on the wall. No canvases or works in progress were anywhere to be seen.

Adrian walked back across the yard and sat in one of the Adirondack chairs and propped his elbows on the wide arms and rested his chin on his folded hands and wondered what to make of the place. Surely, he thought, Ben Walters would be here in midsummer if he was going to be here at all. The place's vacancy had about it a permanence that was, to Adrian, palpable. He figured that Ben Walters, now nearing seventy-five, widowed and alone, his little artistic career having come to nothing, must be summering out in assisted living or a nursing home, probably after the second or third stroke had left him paralyzed or dumbstruck. Anyway, Adrian was sure, Ben was never going to be skippering a sailboat off the coast or walking the beach or sweeping anyone else's wife off her feet, not in this life, and likely not in another. Ben Walters was no longer a man he need contend with. It was good that he'd come here to make this clear.

Adrian tried to imagine how it must have been for Clare. Getting her friend Christine to cover for her, getting here, getting it on with the old fart, the romance of it all, the distance from Findlay, Ohio, the hopes for a new, more exciting life.

She'd gotten as far as Cleveland in the years since. She'd married again and divorced again, and again. She seemed, these long years since, every bit as discontented, only older. The children had each spent hours with counselors learning to love their mother without having to approve of her 'inappropriate choices', and to maintain the proper 'emotional borders' between themselves and their mother's insuperably chaotic life.

It occurred to Adrian that if she outlived him, much of his hard-earned estate would work its way to her, through the generosity of his children, who would surely use a portion of their inheritance to support their mother, who could be counted on to be, as ever, in need.

Oh well, is what he told himself, when such things came to him.

There was nothing about this place, his coming here that had the sense of portent he had imagined when he first made arrangements to come here. He had simply married the wrong woman. He had chosen wrongly. He had mistaken passion and good sex, easy to muster at twenty-something, for true affection. He knew it early in the marriage. He remembered the mornings he would awake beside her, wishing there were more about her that he really treasured, really admired, really needed. She was not, he knew, a great mother, an exceptional human, or a particularly good woman. They had made good babies, not brought out the worst in each other. But neither had they brought out the best. And he had been, stupidly, willing to live with the consequences of his poor decisions, to tolerate waking next to a woman whom he did not truly admire in trade for lovely children and an ordinary life free of the larger vexations. He had not, in his marriage to her, abused her physically or verbally. He had tried his very best to make her happy. He hadn't drank or gambled or cavorted with other women. He'd done his share of diapers and dishes. He had tried to support her efforts to find more interesting things to 'do' than 'wife and mothering'. He had been, in all ways he thought, the reliable husband, the agreeable helpmate, the hedged bet against hunger and loneliness, the other body in the bed. But he had not, he knew it now, ever loved her entirely. Surely that was a critical fault. Sitting in the Adirondack chair on Ben Walters's deserted front lawn, Adrian wondered if she'd ever known how much he really didn't love her. Maybe something in her sensed that emptiness and railed against his willingness to live in a lackluster if otherwise functional marriage. Maybe it was this that drove her to do what she had done. He had been willing to settle for too little. For him it had always seemed sufficient. For her, enough would never be enough. Which aberration of desire, he now wondered, offended God or Nature or the Fates the most? His willingness to settle or her refusal to? His contentment or her discontent?

Here in a clearing in the woods, in the small yard of the small house where the wife of his youth had long ago betrayed him, it all seemed to him like a mystery now, fathomless and unknowable – the ways of the humans and their hearts.

So it was with Mary De Dona. Much as she'd appeared, she disappeared. She simply wasn't there when Adrian returned from his banishment in England. 'You lovely man', is how she addressed the letter she'd left for him with Father Concannon, which thanked him for 'his tenderness and generosities' and gave no further details about her plans or whereabouts. She left brief farewell notes for his children too, in the rooms she'd done up for him in their new residence.

'I couldn't tell you, Adrian, I haven't a clue', the priest insisted under questioning. 'She turned in her keys and resignation and drove off smiling and waving goodbye, that miserable hound in the backseat of the car.'

Adrian was not surprised. He'd come home from west Yorkshire with a finished manuscript, a determination to leave the church, a sense of new message and purpose, and a new place to live in Findlay, Ohio.

He thought he caught a glimpse of Mary De Dona or someone who looked strikingly like her once while he was watching a movie in a hotel room in Minneapolis. Adrian watched and waited for the credits, which listed her name as Sasha Black. Then he lay back on the pillow, fell asleep, and dreamed cinematic dreams. He would search on the Internet but never find her.

He was suddenly worried about missing the boat. He'd lost all track of time somehow.

He jogged back to the car where Gloria was just finishing a cigarette. She pressed it out in the ashtray and started the engine.

'Anyone home?'

'No one, nothing there.'

'Too bad', she said. 'You've come all this way.'

'Oh well', Adrian said. 'Another time maybe.'

She backed out to Pilot Hill Road and drove Adrian back to the ferry docks. He gave her a hundred-dollar bill and thanked her for the tour.

'But it's only thirty dollars.'

'Buy a little cheer for the birthday party.'

'That's really good of you', Gloria said, folding the crisp note into her shirt pocket.

'May I ask you,' Adrian said, leaning back with one foot out of the car, 'may I ask you, Gloria, did you ever find yourself, like ever, in those fifty-eight years, you know, married to Bob, did you ever wonder, What the hell am I doing here? you know with the kids and the work and the routine?'

'No' she said without hesitation, 'never once. I was just so glad to have him home, safe, after the war, I'd missed him so. And I thought, I always thought, what a beautiful man, what a good man he was. So I can tell you, we had our hard days, sure. But no, I never wondered about being with him. I wish I were with him now. I can still feel him.'

There was a catch in her breath. Her hands dropped from the steering wheel of the old wagon. Adrian said nothing.

'The young these days are so unhappy, so impatient, so full of expectations. All we wanted was to survive it. To be together. To get through, Bob and me, you know, and for the children . . . Nowadays they just want too much. Whatever they have, they think there must be more. They want so much they don't know what they want.'

She was staring at a point in the middle of the steering wheel. She caught her breath again.

'Yes, yes, I suppose that's it.'

Adrian wondered what it was he wanted. He had long since lost hope of a woman who could love him like a wife would and love his children like a mother. That mix of passion and sacrifice seemed quite impossible to him now. Not because such women did not exist, but because he lacked what it was they wanted. Though he'd had housekeepers and nannies and tutors and teachers and therapists for his children; though he'd had no shortage of memorable sexual partners; there had not been nor would there be, he now knew with certainty, anyone like Gloria in his life and times – a woman who would mourn and remember the boy he had been, the man he was, the old man he hoped to be, who would love him and outlive him and keep him alive in the daily lives and times of his people, his children and his children's children. He could feel a wave of sadness rising in him that he knew, if he did not move, would overtake him.

He closed the car door and made for the ferry.

'Safe home', she shouted after him.

Boarding the boat, Adrian blew kisses.